Her Wonderful Wonder Belle

A Ghostlight Falls Story

Sylvia Morrow

Contents

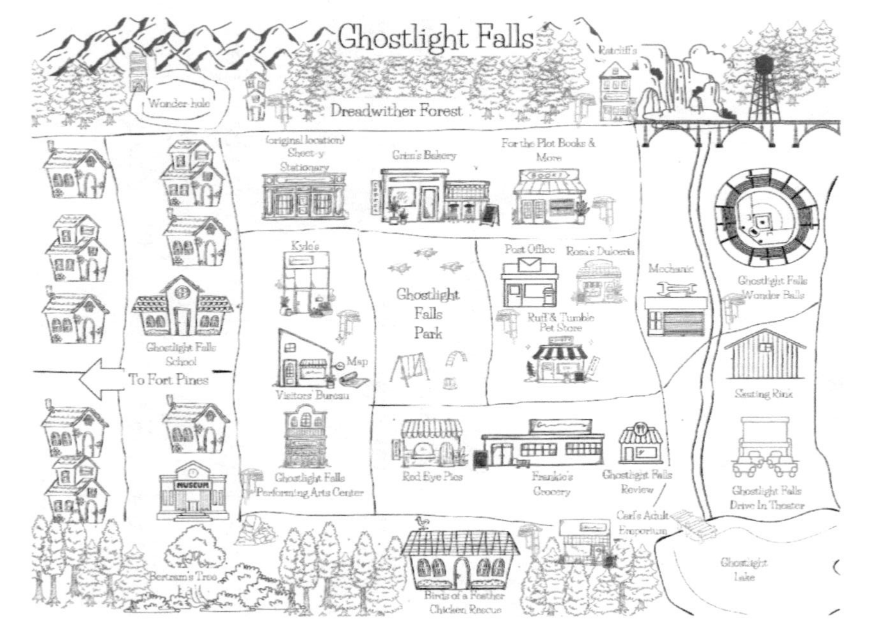

Ghostlight Falls
Wonder hole
Dreadwither Forest
Ratcliff's
(original location)
Sheet-y Stationary
Grim's Bakery
For the Plot Books & More
Kyle's
Post Office
Rosa's Dulceria
Mechanic
Ghostlight Falls Wonder Balls
Ghostlight Falls Park
Ruff & Tumble Pet Store
Ghostlight Falls School
Map
To Fort Pines
Visitors' Bureau
Skating Rink
Ghostlight Falls Performing Arts Center
Red Eye Pies
Frankie's Grocery
Ghostlight Falls Review
Ghostlight Falls Drive In Theater
MUSEUM
Carl's Adult Emporium
Ghostlight Lake
Bertram's Tree
Birds of a Feather Chicken Rescue

Content Notes and What's Inside

This is a modern sapphic love story, but with a historical twist, set in the fictional town of Ghostlight Falls. It's kind of a sentient object story, but also kind of not. It's a little bit historical romance, but also definitely not. The main character really wants it to be a sports romance, but her bad back says no way.

It *is* a lot of fun though. Bring replacement sheets; things will get sticky.

Potential triggers or other concerns:

Discussion of war, including, but not limited to, the 1940s Mediterranean Theater (Italy and Greece specifically.) Mention of experimentation on prisoners. Vague discussion of religion/afterlife. Mention of past religious abuse by a parent. Teenage runaway. Talk of historical and current homophobia and persecution against queer people. Mention of American politics. Getting licked without permission by a stranger. Side character uses a legal recreational vape. Someone disrespecting disabled parking spots. Chronic back pain. Slime. Getting sticky all over. Lots of mentions of chewing/eating. Detailed descriptions of sexual activities. Severe cat-like scratches. Passing mention of bugs. Misogyny. Ableism.

Chapter One

Delia

"Welcome to Ghostlight Falls, the home of friendly weirdos, reasonably priced roadside attractions, and the best minor league baseball team in the country. Enjoy your visit!" I tip my well-worn cap to the out-of-town visitors as they exit the stadium. You can always tell they're not from around here by the slightly confused look in their eyes. Visiting a town full of cryptids, shifters, and other oddballs will do that.

I love living here for so many reasons, but the part about baseball is the biggest. The Wonder Balls are the greatest team in the world, and I get to be part of them—as a custodian, I mean. They don't let women play, obviously. Doesn't matter what role I'm playing though. I'd rather be cleaning after The Wonder Balls than working anywhere else.

Ghostlight Falls Stadium itself has been about the same since it was built almost a hundred years ago, other than technological upgrades and other necessary improvements. The things that are my responsibility to clean—the dugout, locker room, bullpen—all that stuff's stayed the same the whole ten years I've been working here and well before that.

The job itself is...well, if I didn't love baseball so much, I'm not sure I'd still be working here. The work is gross, pay is terrible, my boss is *super* creepy, and a lot of the players are—

"Hey, Dee, you out there?" a man shouts in a half-laugh from inside the locker room.

"No, Brock. Now move your asses. I want to go home!" I yell through the doorway. Brock Ultraman, the star pitcher, is always messing with me. He has ever since we were kids.

"Hold your horses, Delia. We're packing up. Go do something else. Text your boyfriend or whatever."

Boyfriend—no, thank you. He knows I stopped trying to date guys way back when we were teens, but with Brock I can never be sure if it's malice or the fact that he's a fucking moron.

"Whatever, just hurry. I'm waiting on you so I can finish." I pull my grimy, yellow mop bucket against the wall and I lean on the cool stone next to it.

"I like to think of you when I *finish*, Dee," he taunts.

"Brock, you smell like a dirty, infected belly button piercing." I rub my aching lower back. "And don't make me tell the new guys about the time in college when you drank all that pre-workout and shit your pants."

The guys bust out laughing at that. *Got him, ha!* A minute goes by, and the laughs and jokes at Brock's expense grow closer as the guys exit the locker room. Just the last few stragglers after their practice tonight. Brock leads the way, all blonde sunshine with a swagger that says, *"I'll one day be the example of what not to do in a Human Resources training exercise."* He rolls his eyes, flipping me off. A couple guys I don't know that well yet leave next—new to town, they just came on this season—and finally Angelo, currently the only cool guy on the team.

Angelo smiles and pinches his nostrils as he walks out. "Wow, she's right, Brock. You *do* stink. You should see someone about that."

"I'll see your mama on my dick," Brock snaps back.

Everyone pauses.

Idiot. Angelo is a scary as fuck shifter who could toss his ass into the next century, easy.

More importantly though, Angelo's mom is *Rosa*.

"*My* mom?" Angelo asks, hand on his chest and an amused look on his face. His deep brown eyes flash red in the dim hall. "Should I call her and ask her about that? You know, your mom likes to stop by Rosa's for caramels. Maybe *my* mom should ask *your* mom about it."

Everyone likes the candy at Rosa's. It's the best there is anywhere, if you ask me. Having a Candy Witch in Ghostlight Falls is amazing. Pissing her off though? *Terrible* idea. I'm pretty sure that rule number one of living in a town with people who can put curses on you, is *don't do shit that makes them want to put curses on you.*

"I was just kidding." Brock raises his hands, palms forward, and shrugs. "Sorry, man. And, uh, you know I was kidding too, Delia. Right?"

Angelo grins, leans against the wall next to me, and swings his arm around my shoulder. He always smells nice—musky in that "alpha shifter" way—but nice. Being friends with Rosa's kids is just about as sweet as her candy.

"It's all good. Right, Dee?" he asks.

"Yeah," I reply with a wink. I pull away from him and haul my mop bucket toward the now-empty locker room. "Now, get out of here. I need to clean up after your filthy asses so I can get home."

"Have fun," Angelo teases as he pulls off my cap to rub his knuckles quickly back and forth over the top of my head.

"Hey!" I smooth my hair back and fit my cap into place as they all walk out of the building.

I've had the same brown, chin-length hairstyle, with the same bleach-blonde chunks in the front, since I was fourteen. The same year I got this Wonder Balls cap, two years before I started working here. The stadium and I have that in common—we don't change much. I mean, a little change would be nice. Like, maybe a new girlfriend. It's hard to find another chick around here who's as into baseball as I am though—and she *does* need to be into it. I've tried dating people who didn't like the sport. It didn't go well. They could only listen to me ramble on about stats and player trades so much before they got bored.

Ah, well. Someday. Right now, I need to be thinking less about pretty gals, and more cleaning out garbage pails. Time to get to work.

"Rogers!" a deep, gravely voice echoes from the far end of the hall. *My boss*. Garbage pails will have to wait a second.

"Yes, Mr. Brigley?" I shout as I drop my mop, jogging toward him. He doesn't like slow movers.

His massive silhouette darkens the light of the arch at the end of the hallway tunnel. Brigley has to be close to seven feet tall. He's pure muscle, but not in the bodybuilding way. Those bodybuilders look tough, but it's mostly for show. They're just the muscle head version of beauty pageant contestants. Guys like Brigley—the ones that have massive barrel chests with hair that pokes out of the collars of their shirts, and hands the size of catcher's mitts—those are the real strong men. You don't wanna mess with them.

"You got overtime Wednesday," he barks when I get close enough to make out his features.

Ashes from his cigar drop to the floor. This hall isn't my area to clean, but it's still annoying to watch. Janitor solidarity.

"Oh, I took that day off because my—"

"Did I ask you a question, Rogers?"

The shadows in the archway start to close in around me. The edges of them twist in unnatural ways that make my stomach twist just as much. I swallow the last of the saliva I have as I my mouth goes dry.

"No, Sir."

"I didn't think so." His walrus-like mustache twitches as he gives me a long, silent look.

He drops his cigar and stamps it out. I force myself not to look away as he takes a piece of gum from his pocket, opens it, throws the wrapper on the floor, and puts the gum in his mouth.

"Be here at six."

"Yes, Sir."

The shadows retreat as he lumbers away to his office—far the fuck away from me, thank goodness. I shiver as the blood returns to my body and my system starts functioning properly again. Most days I don't have to deal with Brigley, but when I do...*ugh*.

Anyway, back to work.

They left the locker room surprisingly tidy today. Not even a single jockstrap flung into the sink, and no one shaved their pubes on the floor. What a win.

I make progress fast tonight, shaking my behind while I scrub the showers to my choice of music. I try not to let anyone see me dance. I have limbs like an antelope, the posture of a croissant, and a complete lack of rhythm. My whole dance routine gives "ostrich mating ritual." Might be another reason I'm single.

When I'm done in the locker room, I take the mop bucket back to the janitor's area and dump it. That's it for the night. I wash my hands and grab my backpack from the employee lockers.

Finally, I can go home, eat some food, power up the PC and play Ultra Baseball MVP VII. My bad back might keep me from playing ball (when an accident gave me a spine that looks like a depressed shrimp it put a dent in things), but video games? Hell yeah. Gamers and terrible postures are built for each other.

Hmm. The staying in the house and playing games all the time could *also* be part of the reason I'm single.

I'm most of the way out of the building, nearly free to hit pixel balls, when I stumble in the hall.

Pain races up my bones as I hit the floor, elbows first. *Oof.*

Eyes shut tight, I grimace until the initial shock of the fall passes. When I open them, I spot a loose brick under me. Why we still have brick floors in the hallway, no clue, but they're annoying. Pretty sure it's just because they're old like the rest of the building. They're a bitch to clean, and apparently a tripping hazard too.

I'm about to stand up when I notice something out of place—and shiny—underneath the brick. After moving it aside, I take my keys out of my bag and use one as a little shovel to dig the metal thing out.

It takes a bit, but soon enough I pull out a small box.

Once it's free, I fit the brick back into place as best as I can, slip the box into my backpack, and head out the door. I have no clue what this is, but there's no way I'm turning it in to my boss.

As I'm walking home, I hear fans chant "Balls! Balls! Balls!" from inside Kyle's pub, and it makes me think of what Brigley might do if he knew I took something from the stadium without permission. I shudder to imagine it. I mean, it's not like I've ever *seen* him do anything terrible to someone. Outside of his duties as owner and coach of the Wonder Balls, I've only ever *seen* him smoke cigars, chew gum, and lurk ominously. If anyone knew for a fact he did any of the things he's been *rumored* to have done, then he'd be in jail. It's just that bad things have a way of mysteriously happening after he gets mad. More than a couple of people who pissed him off up and left Ghostlight Falls in the middle of the night, without telling anyone, and without ever speaking to anyone ever again.

So, I'm *not* going to tell anyone where I found this box.

When I get to my place, I lock the door behind me and set my bag on the purple sofa (that I got for free off of the curbside, by the way—I'm still proud of that score.) I kick my chunky, black boots off near the entryway while pulling my work uniform shirt off. Slipping and sliding in my socks on the wood floors, I make my way to my bedroom where I toss the clothes into the hamper. The doom pile of clean, un-folded laundry leers at me from the chair beside my bed. Really need to fold those someday... Not today.

I grab one of my many silly t-shirts and pull it over my head. Today's tee has a cartoon rat on the front and says "God of Lust" on top and "Be Like Him" on the bottom. Does it make sense? No, but I got it for two dollars at the Ghost-light Falls thrift store, and it makes me smile. After tugging on a pair of baggy gray sweat-pants, I head back to the living room to retrieve the briefly forgotten box before returning to the bedroom, so I lounge in bed while checking it out.

I wipe the grime off the box using my trusty bedside baby wipes then get to work trying to open it. The top of it is pitted and worn, but it's not rusted or anything. I can make out faded paint with the logo of Rosa's Dulcería. It looks way too old to have been owned by the Rosa I know, but the candy store has been around longer with that name than she has. The two halves of the box are jammed together pretty hard. Every way I pull is stuck. I grumble with irritation, about to throw the damn thing.

"Please just freaking open," I say between gritted teeth as I tug again.

The box pops open. *Score!* And...it's anti-climactic. There isn't much inside. A yellowing piece of paper. An empty gum wrapper. A base-ball card. The piece of paper has some writing on it, but it's short, and pretty confusing.

To whoever finds this-

If you're reading this, then only you can help. This gal needs a lot of it. Help, that is. Please take care of her.

If Brigley is still around when you find this, DO NOT trust him! DO NOT tell him she—or any of the girls—are back!

-V

Brigley? As in Mister Brigley, my boss, *owner* of the Wonder Balls? She can't be talking about the same guy. The man I know is older than me, yeah, but he's not old enough to have been around when Rosa's grandma wrote that. At least, that's who I'm guessing V is, anyway, since Valentina owned the candy store before Rosa. She was old when I was born and dead since I was a little kid.

Oh, I'm so dumb—they must be talking about Brigley's dad. Or even grandpa? I don't know anything about his family, but it would make sense.

As for the rest of the letter, what the hell does that mean? Who am I supposed to take care of, and why would I be the only one who could take care of them? How would a candy store owner from way back know who would find this?

Actually, this whole thing was probably left as a prank or something. A joke that they expected someone to find sooner. *Hmm.*

Well, onto the more exciting part—the baseball card. I *love* baseball cards. I especially love *rare* baseball cards, and I've never seen one like this. It's clearly old because it's in black and white, first off, and they started regularly producing color photograph cards in the fifties. Second, this is a card featuring a player from the North American Ladies Baseball League, which went under in 1952.

Wait. The North American Ladies Baseball League never had baseball cards. They didn't get treated with that kind of respect.

I read the card carefully.

Pearl Monroe

North American Ladies Baseball League All Star

Pitcher—Ghostlight Falls Wonder Belles—1943-1946

Wait, what? Ghostlight Falls had a women's baseball team? That can't be right. I've read everything I could find on our town's baseball history ever since I learned to read. Not once was anything named Wonder *Belles* mentioned. It's Wonder *Balls.* Always has been.

I read the card again and again, but it doesn't give me any further hints about the team, only a blurb about the player, Pearl.

"Pearl Monroe is famous for her ability to pitch and bat both left and right-handed with equal skill. While much of her childhood remains a mystery, her early adult years were spent with the glitterati. Though she's best known for her films such as "Funny Broad" and "One Night in Ontario," she's also done charity work by filming public service warnings for schools like "Reefer Goons, Get Lost!" and "Pants On, Books Open."

Well, that's...outdated.

I look at the picture again. The face of Pearl Monroe smiles at me. She's really beautiful. Anyone could tell by looking that she's hamming it up for the camera.

In those days they made women wear skirts while playing, and she's posing in a way that shows just a little more leg than strictly necessary. She's got this big, cheeky smile while holding the bat, the kind of expression you'd see on the old pin-up art. Her light blonde ponytail, poking out the back of her red cap, is curled perfectly at the end. Somehow, even though it's in black and white, I can tell that the dark tint of her lips is red. Damn, she's hot. No wonder she got a baseball card back when no other ladies did.

"I wish I had a pretty girlfriend like her who liked baseball as much as I do," I mumble.

Ugh. Maybe I'm a little lonelier than I thought because now I just feel sad. There really isn't anyone like this Pearl girl around here. Fucking woe is me.

I set the box and card on my bed. Turning on the computer to get it ready to game, I put a background show on the T.V. and leave the room. In the kitchen, I grab a cold drink of water to reset my system. No use in sitting around dehydrated and feeling sad about girls when I have technology to numb my brain.

As I head back toward my room, I hear a rustling sound coming from inside. It's not loud but there's definitely movement. From the hallway, I creep closer toward the open door. I'd grab my bat to protect myself, but of course I left it under my bed.

Please don't kill me before I beat the game. I haven't even unlocked all the stadiums yet.

My heart pounds as I poke my head just barely inside. What horrible creature might be waiting there to maim me?

Holy Fucking Balls.

Pearl Monroe is standing in my bedroom, in full color, *alive*...ish.

I'm pretty sure she's talking to me, but I can't hear what she's saying. I'm too busy processing the fact that she's made of fucking *paper*.

Chapter Two

Pearl

"**M**a'am? Excuse me? Ma'am? Can you tell me where I am?"

I wave my hand in front of the gal's face, but she continues to stare blankly at me. There must be something wrong with her.

I raise my voice in case she can't hear me. "Are you alright? Do you need help?"

Her mouth opens and closes as if she intends to reply, but she still says nothing. How frustrating. Maybe there *is* something wrong.

She's a strange-looking woman. She's got stripes in her hair like that Bride of Franken-stein film. Tattoos poke out from under those men's gym clothes she's wearing. Goodness, she even has metal rings through her lip and nose!

She must be some sort of performer with those looks, certainly.

"Ma'am are you with the circus? A traveling show of some kind?" I ask hopefully. Surely someone could help me from an entire carnival full of people.

She only looks more confused. Sighing, I look around the room for answers instead.

Oh boy. There are lights flickering and images glowing from machines all over the room. I'm not sure what's going on, but I don't think I like it. I know there's been a visitor or two to Ghostlight Falls from beyond the stars, but they've sworn not to take us away unwillingly. I'm going to be so very upset if I'm on some other planet.

Something on a table next to me shakes, then lights up, revealing a glowing photograph of a men's baseball team in full color. It continues to vibrate, the words "Mom Calling" across the top. None of this makes any kind of sense. Why would an alien have baseball? Or their words be in English?

"I don't like this. Just tell me where I am." I can hear the shakiness of distress in my voice.

Normally I prefer to be the knight in shining armor, but I suppose this time I'm the damsel. Well, I guess my show of emotion gives the tattooed lady a kick in the behind, because she finally answers me.

"You're in my room. In, uh, Ghostlight Falls. Do you—you do realize that you're—" She claps her hands flat together like she's praying, looking at me as if that's supposed to mean something.

"Well, first off, thank you for *finally* answering me. Who may I ask are you? And if I'm in *your* room, *why* am I here? Also, I must say I don't know what you're trying to say with that clap." I mimic her gesture and am surprised to find that I make no sound.

I look down at my hands and freeze. Something is very, very wrong here.

"Do you see what I mean?" the woman asks.

"I see something. Don't know what," I say with some difficulty.

"Paper," she says, as if that makes any kind of sense.

I look at her and wait for a saner response.

"You're made of paper. I think. At least, you were made of paper a couple of minutes ago."

That really isn't any saner.

"What are you talking about? I feel normal."

I hold my hands in front of my face and—*well, shit.* I look down at my legs and any other part of me I can see. Everything's flat.

It's true, I'm all paper.

"I don't understand. My brain's working, my heart's beating. I'm moving around, and I really do feel just fine. How can this be real?"

"I don't know. Why don't you sit down, and I'll tell you what I *do* know." She gestures to a chair with a bunch of clothes on it, which she swiftly moves to the floor. "My name's Delia, by the way."

I sit on the chair, nodding in her direction as I do. "Pleasure meeting you. I'm Pearl."

"Well, Pearl, let me tell you what I know about how you got here."

A few minutes later I'm just about as stumped as I was before. I didn't know Valentina well, but she was a nice woman. Always willing to help a girl in need.

Brigley was nice *before* the war. He inherited the gum factory and used the money to buy the men's baseball team, the Wonder Balls. When he went to war, and most of the men in town did too, the Wonder Belles took over for the Balls.

After Brigley got back something changed in him. He was real mean. At first, people thought he maybe had some kind of shell shock or something. That happened to some guys, they got irritable when they returned. Battle fatigue did all kinds of awful things to our boys, but this was different. Darker. Saying not to trust Brigley is the least surprising thing about all of this.

"And you don't remember how you got in your current...condition at all?" Delia asks.

"I really don't. I remember our team captain, Cheryl, phoning me for an emergency meeting. And that's the last thing I recall." I try again to think of anything after I hung up the phone that evening, but there's just nothing else. "How long has it been, by the way? You didn't say."

"Oh. I don't know how long it's been since you were—whatever happened to you, but it's twenty-twenty-five now."

"I must be misunderstanding. You don't mean the *year* twenty-twenty-five?"

"Yeah. It's been almost eighty years since you were on that card." Delia nervously bites the metal ring on her lip.

"The last year I remember is 1946. I missed all that time. Did anyone look for me?"

She slowly shakes her head. "There wasn't anything about this town even having a women's team on record. If there was, I would have found it."

"Someone must have erased us. But why? And now I'm here all alone where I don't belong." I look down at my hands. They're freakish. "Am I even me?"

"I'm so sorry, Pearl."

"Meow! Pbft!"

My eyes dart to the window where a fluffy, gray face stares at me. The fluffy little beast opens its mouth wide and pats the screen with one white-booted paw. *"Meow!"*

"Mavis! There you are!" Delia crawls across her bed to the window to let the cat inside. It struts into the room, fluffy tail held high, rubbing on her owner and meowing loudly over and over. "She escaped out the window this morning and I couldn't find her. I knew she'd come back though. She always does."

Delia rubs her nose against the cat's nose, making happy cooing noises. Mavis sneezes directly into Delia's open eye.

"Eew, thanks Mavis," Delia groans as she sits up, wiping her face on the end of her t-shirt.

Briefly, I see her stomach. She even has a tattoo there, too! I look away too quickly to make out what it is, but I can't help but be curious. Strangely, I must admit the secret tattoo on her flat stomach, in those masculine pants, gives me feelings I don't really need to be having right now. Maybe I'm all confused in the head from the strange events of the day. I certainly shouldn't be thinking about sex at a time like this.

The cat jumps off the bed and walks over to me. I do love animals, and this one is particularly adorable. Its ears are long and hanging low like a bunny's, which I've never seen on a cat before.

"You know, the Wonder Belles had a cat named Tubbs. Well, he lived outside, but we called him ours. He sat on the porch of the house where a group of us single gals lived every morning, and we'd scratch his little white head before every game for luck." I scratch the top of Mavis's head. "Are you lucky, Mavis?"

"*Pbft*," she replies, a very strange sound for a cat.

"Oh, she's not a cat. She's a *cant*. I got her at Ruff 'N Tumble. They sell exotic pets. I got her because she's awesome at fetch."

The cant starts to knead my shoe as if she's making biscuits, but since the shoe is made of paper, it just sort of crinkles noisily. Mavis jumps back, confused. Her pupils grow wide, and her long ears flip backward.

"Oh. She doesn't look exotic. Cute, just not exotic." I tilt my head and watch the grey fluff ball watching my shoe.

To my amazement, an additional, long, skinny, almost spider-like leg, with sharp claws on the end, shoots out of each side of Mavis's body. Before I can even figure out whether to scream or piddle myself, she springs forward and slashes her claws right through my shoe.

"Mavis!" Delia shrieks as she launches off of the bed.

She grabs the cant and slides her into the hallway, slamming the door behind her.

She kneels before me, inspecting my shoe. "Oh shit, are you okay?"

"I don't know. It didn't hurt but it doesn't look good."

My paper has several tears where Mavis's claws shredded it. Everything below my left ankle is tattered ribbons, dangling in the still air. Thinking about it is making me nauseous.

"What if we tape you back together?" Delia asks, eyes wide with hope.

"Tape? As in Scotch tape? Oh boy, do I feel silly."

"Just let me try, okay?" Delia scurries over to one of the desks where the disturbingly glowing machines sit.

She pulls out a roll of clear tape, returns, then begins to very carefully put me back as I was.

"What are those things on the desk? The glowing things?" I ask. Might as well find out in case I'm in danger.

"Oh, uh, there are a few different things. The big, flat one with the movie playing on mute right now, that's the television. And—"

"That can't be a television. I was an actress, did you know that? Sometimes I'd get offers from people who wanted me to return to the screen. Once a gentleman in television invited me to his home to show me the latest devices. They looked nothing like that." I laugh at the thought. If we had to do our hair and makeup to be in pictures like *that*, then some of the gals I worked with would quit. You can see the pores in their skin! They already grumbled enough about Technicolor.

"You forget that it's been eighty years, Pearl. Technology has changed. Makeup technology too."

"Oh, right." I laugh to try to cover up my embarrassment. "Well, what about that other thing. The smaller one?"

"That's my computer. I mostly play games on it, but it can do a lot of stuff. Honestly, I don't even know where to start. I'd have to explain the Internet first, I think." Delia closes her eyes and takes a deep breath. "Wow, where to begin?"

"Alright, well, what is the computer itself? You can start there. I know a television is for watching shows, but I'm not understanding what a computer is. I've heard the word, but I don't know how it applies to games and nets."

"It's—okay, you see, when you—uh, fuck, I have no idea how to explain a computer. You just turn on the power and type and it does a bunch of stuff...I don't know. That's not my area of expertise."

She scrunches up her face in clear embarrassment before letting out a laugh that has a hint of a sea lion bark to it. It's such an odd laugh that I can't help but to laugh in return.

She shakes her head at me. "Why are you laughing?"

"You sound a bit like Sparky, the sea lion I worked with on the film 'Here Comes Mister Fish!' I won an award for that one."

"Hey!" Her eyebrows pinch inward as she frowns. "Don't make fun of my laugh."

"I'm not making fun. Well, not too much fun. I like your laugh." I rest two flat fingers under her chin and look her directly in her lovely green eyes. "I think you're sweet, Delia. You've got pretty peepers too."

Fast as can be her face turns hot, red as the devil's underwear. My goodness. When I pull my hand away, I can see her pulse racing in her long, thin neck. Her eyes have stayed locked on mine, but her pupils have certainly grown.

She slides the edge of her thumb along the thin side of my hand without looking away from me for even a second. Her voice has a breathless quality to it when she says, "No papercut. Nice."

My goodness indeed. Delia here has a crush on me, despite my dimensional predicament. I clear my throat. Back in my day the good citizens of Ghostlight Falls were very clear about how we felt about that sort of thing. She didn't tell me how long she's been living here; she may be new to town for all I know. I don't know if she knows our ways. Best she knows now how things work around here.

"Delia. I need to ask you something. Be honest." I smooth the skirt of my light pink baseball uniform and straighten my posture. "Are you—well, do you play for the *other team*? If you understand."

Delia only looks confused. "I have no idea what you mean. I *work* at the Wonder Balls stadium; I don't actually play baseball."

"No. I mean—well, I'll just say it. Honey, are you queer? It's alright to tell me. You have my full support."

Delia starts laughing so hard she falls backward. She lays on her back until her laughs turn into coughs. I, on the other hand, do not find it amusing in the slightest.

"I don't see why it's funny. I'm asking a serious question. If you aren't willing to answer, that's fine, I understand, and apologize for overstepping. I do not, however, apologize for taking the subject seriously."

"I just didn't expect it," she replies, out of breath.

She sits back up, her expression much more appropriate. "It's not really something you blurt out to people you've just met, you know? I didn't mean to make you feel bad. Oh, I finished with your shoe by the way."

I look at my foot and see that it's taped back together quite well. Obviously, you can see the tape, but Delia matched up the torn places seamlessly. I flex my foot, and everything moves together just fine. An extra crunchy sound from the cellophane, but nothing I can't tolerate.

"Why, thank you! It really worked!"

"No problem!" She grins wide before squinting sheepishly. "And yes, I'm queer. I'm happily gay and everyone around here knows it. Does that bother you?"

"Absolutely not. I asked because I wanted you to know that you're supported. We accept everyone who accepts us in Ghostlight Falls, and don't tolerate the horrible bigotry of outsiders." I tip my head to the side as I think. "At least, that's how it used to be. It was one of the main reasons I moved here. I came for a Wonder Balls game with a friend and saw all the different types of couples out in the open, everyone accepting them, treating them equally. When I saw they were having tryouts for the Wonder Belles, I moved here on a bus with a one-way ticket. I certainly hope it hasn't changed. Would be a tragedy if things grew hateful here."

"Oh, heck no. Ghostlight Falls is just about the most accepting place there is. As long as you support the Wonder Balls and not the Ankara Eels, of course." Delia winks.

The Ankara Eels have been the rivals of the Wonder Balls since before my time. When there's a Balls versus Eels game happening, the whole town gets riled up.

"Well, of course. No one likes an Eels fan. If you're not a Wonder Balls fanatic, are you even really a citizen here?"

I put my hand over my heart and begin to sing the one song everyone in Ghostlight Falls knows—The Wonder Balls anthem. Delia stands to join me shortly after I begin.

There's never any wonder
Who's the best team in the Falls
They'll never steal our thunder
Cuz we're the Wonder Balls!

From hole to lake to forest
We fight for Ghostlight Falls
We'll never give them rest
Cuz we're the Wonder Balls!

Balls! Balls! Balls!
We're gonna fight! Fight! Fight!
For the Falls! Falls! Falls!
B-A-L-L BALLS! Go Balls!

I clasp my hands together in delight. "It's good to know some things stay the same."

"For sure." Delia's smiling eyes turn curious when they dart back down to my shoe. "So, question. Did your foot get sliced up too? It couldn't have been just your shoe, right?"

"What do you mean? Clearly not. I think I would feel it if my foot were torn up."

"Yeah, but Mavis sliced through the whole piece of paper. I mean, you. Shoe, sock, foot. The whole thing was shredded, and I taped it back together. How did you not feel it?"

"Oh my. I didn't stop to think about it. Haven't really stopped to think about much. There's a lot happening." I wiggle my foot again. It seems fine. "I suppose I could take off the shoe and check."

My stomach feels like it's twisting in knots with how nervous I am about it. I bend over and take a close look, pursing my lips in concentration. How am I supposed to untie a two-dimensional shoe? *Hmm.* Here we go.

As odd as it looks, the action itself goes quite smoothly. It's so surreal though because to me, everything feels normal—I'm untying a shoe, same as always. Nothing is off about it to me except the annoying rustling sound I make when I move. In fact, I notice that when I move my clothing it moves smoothly along with me, but when an outside force attempts to, it's stiff. How strange and frustrating.

"Wow, that looks crazy. It's like—actually, I was gonna say it's like you're a moving photograph, but that's pretty much what you are, so that would be stupid to say. It's like I'm watching one of those life-sized stand-up displays of movie stars they have at the theater sometimes, you know? Except alive. A moving photo with a soul," Delia says, rapid-fire thoughts spilling out, as she's watching me slip off my taped-together paper shoe.

It turns out there's an entirely whole, stocking-covered paper foot underneath. No tape.

"A soul, huh? My mama wasn't so sure I had a soul. She tried to marry me off to some old preacher when I was fourteen. To save my soul she said. More like to fill her wallet. I packed a bag in the middle of the night, took a train to California, and never saw her again." I turn the shoe over in my hands and inspect the back of it.

My jaw tightens as years of terrible memories before Ghostlight Falls come rushing back. Closing my eyes, I let out a breath, feeling my muscles relax. "I don't know what happened to get me here, but I know I had enough of *something*—essence, spirit, maybe even a *soul*—to save for eighty years, so I could come back as sweet, and kind, and *queer* as I ever was. Looks like my mama was *wrong*."

"Man, fuck your mom." Delia throws a pillow against the wall. "What a bitch."

I bark out a surprised laugh. "Well, that's straight to the point."

"Nothing else to say about it. She was wrong. And a *bitch*." Delia leans back on her elbows, her shirt riding up enough to show a sliver of skin that gets my heart speeding up. "So, anyway, it's too late to go anywhere tonight.

First thing in the morning, though, we need to get to Rosa's. If anyone knows what to do, it's her."

"I'd like to find a way to get some new clothes as well, if possible. I might be made of paper, but I don't want to be in my uniform forever. Oh, and certainly some new stompers—can't be seen in ones held together by tape. A little vain, I know." I brush off my skirt and cross my legs; I can't help being the way I am.

"I got you. Nothing I love more than taking a pretty girl shopping." Delia grins. *Well, my heart may have skipped a beat.* "But for now, I have a question."

She leans forward and I lean toward her in return. *I hope it's something real exciting.* She bites the ring on her lip and wiggles her eyebrows before asking the most confusing thing I've ever heard.

"If I can figure out how to get two-player to work on the PC, do you want to play Ultra Baseball MVP VII with me?"

Chapter Three

Pearl

"H*urry up and chew, you're running out of time."*

The remaining girls from the team and I sit in the locker room with the lights turned off, only a half-hidden flashlight on a bench to see by. We can't let anyone know we're here. We speak in whispers and move as little as possible. Many of the girls have already disappeared. I couldn't tell you who, though—their names are already gone.

"Remember, once the sugar is gone, put the gum back in the wrapper. We need wrapper, gum, card, and letter all in the box," Valentina says only just loud enough for us all to hear.

"He'll be here in two hours. I need to get these boxes buried before then. If he catches me—" Ricky says softly to Valentina. Her husband, a human

contractor at the stadium. He's laying new brick-work in the halls today.

"He won't." She lays a hand on his chest and a kiss on his cheek before turning back to us. "Are you broads finished, or what?"

The sugar is almost gone from my bub-blegum, but not quite. I don't understand how her magic works; gosh, I haven't even known magic existed for long, but I'm trusting it with my life. It's either that or give up and let Brigley take it.

"I'm done," Cheryl says as she frantically wraps her gum in its wrapper. She puts it in the metal candy box Valentina gave each of us next to her baseball card and hands it to the Candy Witch.

"Team captain, of course you'd be first." Valentina smiles. "You're a good woman, Cheryl. I'll make sure your babies are taken care of."

Cheryl lets out a deep sob as she drops to her knees. She has two little boys with no father to take care of them. They'll have no one at all in a few moments.

Valentina wipes away a tear and puts one of the identical letters she's written into the box.

Next, she puts on the metal lid and squeezes it closed as tightly as she can.

Cheryl disappears.

I was told it would happen but it's still a shock. I nearly choke on my gum in surprise but manage to cough it back up. Except I swallow it right back down out of reflex. Damn.

I'm about to ask for another piece, or what else I can do, when I hear muffled cries of terror coming from the girls around me. Another one of us, her name already lost, has disappeared. Not because of Valentina, but because Brigley's curse took her. My stomach lurches so hard I nearly throw the gum back up. Fuck this.

I shove the gum wrapper under my baseball card and hope Valentina won't notice it's empty. Maybe this will work. I mean, the gum is still technically here, right?

"Okay, I'm done. Me next," I say as I rush toward her.

"Alright, Pearl." She puts the letter in the box, and I sigh, relieved she didn't notice the lack of gum. "If anyone can make it back, it's you. If you end up in the future, take a ride in a flying car for me."

"Oh boy, I'm sure I won't be in there long. You'll see me before your hair turns gray." I give her a wave and my signature Pearl Monroe wink as she picks up the lid.

Here we go. To the future.

I wake up, breathing heavily. It came back—my memory. Everything that happened. All the horrible details. I toss aside the covers and stumble out of bed. I'm so dizzy I only make it a few steps before falling over. A sob breaks free as I curl up, wailing loudly, crying for all I've lost.

"Pearl! Pearl, are you okay?" Delia asks as she runs into the room, falls to her knees in front of me. She strokes my cheeks and looks me over for signs of injury. "Baby, are you hurt? What happened?"

"Brigley didn't just kill them, Delia. He erased them. Like they never existed. They don't even have names. I can't tell you anything about them. There are blank spots, and I only know that there was someone there because I watched them as they disappeared. I watched so many girls disappear. Just *gone*." I sob so hard I choke, then I sob some more.

Delia strokes my back. She doesn't tell me it'll be okay, or any of that nonsense. I appreciate it, because for those girls, it'll never be okay, and I just want a moment to grieve.

After a long while, I quiet down enough to speak again.

"I think some of the girls might still be alive. Buried under the bricks like I was. Not many, but a handful. We have to save them."

Delia takes me by the arms and lifts me to a sitting position. She places her hands on my shoulders gently, so she doesn't crumple me, and looks me dead in the eyes.

"If this is somehow my Brigley, and he's as dangerous as you say, then digging up his stadium and reviving people he wanted to ultra-kill is going to get my ass cooked."

My shoulders slump. I know I shouldn't ask her to put her life in danger for people she doesn't know—and who might not even be there.

"But I will absolutely do this. Not just for you, by the way. Though, I am very much hoping I'll get a nice reward when it's done." She offers me a mischievous smile that instantly puts me in a better mood.

"There will be a fantastic reward, I promise," I purr into her ear.

Delia does this throaty half laugh that just about kills me.

"Perfect." She pulls away enough so that I can see her face has turned more serious again. "But I also want to help those other women. I'd never leave another team member behind like that, even if rescue has taken a little longer than ideal."

"Just a *little* longer," I scoff.

She rolls her eyes when Mavis meows loudly outside the door. As she stands up, she pulls me with her. "Let's just get up for the day. I'm not gonna go back to sleep and apparently Mavis wants to eat early."

I eye the door warily. We've kept the cant away from me since the shoe incident. Delia pats me on the back.

"It'll be fine, Pearl. Get dressed. We'll go shopping."

Chapter Four

Delia

Pearl took a really long time to figure out the basics of Ultra Baseball MVP VII, which I expected—she's starting from zero on video game know-how. She got really, really into it once she figured it out, however, which I did not expect. She still doesn't understand what a computer is—not that I've done a good job explaining it, so that's on me—but she's getting pretty damn good at that game.

We stayed up way too late playing, talking about her time with the Wonder Belles, and about when she was in movies. She's so fucking cool. She just about lost her shit—in a good way—when I showed her I could stream pretty much any song she requested, aside from a few obscure ones I just couldn't locate. She tried to get me to get up and dance, but I couldn't make myself. No way am I ruining my chances with the most beautiful woman I've ever seen by dancing like an angry orangutan to Glenn Miller.

I let her sleep in my bed while I slept on the sofa with Mavis's heavy butt, despite Pearl's insistence that it was alright if I slept next to her. I just wanted to be chivalrous and all that, but damn if I didn't think about taking her up on the offer.

When she woke up the way she did I was terrified. She's only been here a matter of hours and already it's like, I don't know; if she was hurt I'd be fucking devastated. Then she shared her memory and things got scary as shit. The information she shared this morning was...well, we're in trouble. I definitely doubled up on the energy drinks this morning, I'll say that much. Gotta be on the alert.

"Holy mackerel! Look at the size of the truck! Must have a load of dough to get one of those." Pearl chatters on as she strolls down the sidewalk, eyes wide at every new thing we pass by. "Jeez, there sure are a lot of people just running everywhere! Where are they going?"

She has more weight to her than I expected, which is good. She's a nice, thick paper stock—more paperback book cover than pages if I had to describe it, I guess. Heavy enough that she can walk without flopping over. That's step one of leaving the house covered. Step two is getting her not to blow away whenever there's a strong gust of wind. We have to work that one out. For now, I'm holding her hand—*oh no, what a shame, whatever will I do*—and thankful that the air is mostly still.

"They run because they want to. For health reasons, usually. Sometimes just for fun." I shrug as another early morning jogger passes by us. "Lots of reasons."

"That's a hobby I certainly don't think I'll be participating in. We do laps for punishment on the team, not recreation."

As we walk out of my quiet residential neighborhood, toward the main part of town, we begin to encounter more people. Some of the older residents give us a wave and barely look twice. Ghostlight Falls has seen weirder. Younger folks, however, are more curious.

"Um, Delia. Is your friend totally flat or was there something weird in my vape? I know I shouldn't order from sketchy sites since it's legal in Oregon. I'm a sucker for a discount, though," my sort-of friend, Janis, says as I walk past the performing arts center.

Janis is a starving artist-type that used to work with me at the stadium. We made out a few times. She left to help teach acting part-time to little kids. I'm happy for her. Honestly, not really sure what she does with the rest of her time. Kind of a mystery, that one.

"She is very much two-dimensional. You're fine. We're on our way to Rosa's to figure out what's going on. You really shouldn't order from those sites, though." I wave goodbye as we continue on past the fancy, old building.

Janis gives me a salute, then hits her vape. Shaking my head with a laugh, I turn to Pearl and find a horrified expression on her face.

"What's wrong?"

"A goof burner, Delia?" she asks under her voice with the tone of a disappointed mother.

"A what?"

"I could smell *reefer* on her. You have got to be careful. There's all sorts of trouble with that type. I did a movie on it." Pearl's look of genuine concern is the only thing keeping me from bursting into laughter.

I swallow down the laughs and do my best to hide my smile. I'll have to remember to give her a talk about this later. "Thanks Pearl."

The walk is long and most of the businesses are new to Pearl, though a lot of the buildings themselves are the same. She's unimpressed by the way cars look these days compared to how they used to look. She says they're too big and fast. To be honest, she's not wrong. The weirdest thing to her, however, is how people carry their phones everywhere.

"Why is everyone staring at those things? You said it's a phone, but I don't see them talking."

We walk through the park and see people laying in the grass or sitting against trees, but almost all of them are scrolling on their smartphones. I wouldn't have noticed it if she hadn't said anything.

"They're not *just* phones. They have the Internet, games, texting, social media, streaming, and other stuff. People use them for work even. There's so much stuff it's hard to explain. I'll have to sit down with you and physically show you because just talking about it isn't gonna cut it."

"I guess you'll have to because a lot of that sounds like gobbledygook." She sighs. "I'm sure I'll have to spend a lot of time learning new things."

"Yeah." I give her hand a reassuring, very gentle squeeze as we continue to walk. "Oh, hey, want to know something fun? The government sent a man to the moon."

"Oh, we've had people who could space travel in Ghostlight Falls for ages. The rest of the country didn't know, but I suppose it's nice that everyone else can do it. Have they made it out of the galaxy? Or made homes up there?" She looks at me with an excited look that has my brain making a disappointed *womp-womp* sound inside.

"No, not yet."

"Oh, shame. I'm sure they will soon. The government must be halfway there by now. You can always rely on them to be on top of things."

"...Yeah."

We make it to Rosa's just after opening. Her daughter, Sharon, is cleaning the counter when we walk in. She's a *very* hot goth babe with long, black hair, elaborate black makeup, and clothes like a Victorian widow. We made a brief attempt at dating, but discovered we were sexually incompatible. It's not impossible for two tops to be together by any means—it happens all the time—but these two tops just didn't work out. Plus, she's not a sports fan, and I don't like the feeling of velvet.

"What do you want?" Sharon asks with her signature monotone voice.

"Actually, we're hoping Rosa is around. We have an issue." I point to Pearl, who waves her hand in an especially flappy way to show off its flatness.

"I'll ask her if she has time. Only because she likes you." She sets down her cleaning supplies and eyes Pearl. "And because of your issue. Lock the front door."

Sharon disappears behind the pink, velvet, rose-printed curtains that hang behind the counter while I lock the door. Pearl and I wait nervously, looking around at the goodies. The place smells like caramel, chocolate, and cinnamon. The décor is pink, red, and deep brown, with roses printed on almost everything.

"Hello, honey. What's going on?" Rosa asks as she walks through the curtain. When she sees Pearl she pauses, looks her up and down, and shakes her head. "Dios mío. It's something new everyday in this town."

"Yep." I chuckle and watch as Pearl blushes with nerves. "As you can see, we have a problem."

"Come back to my office, tell me about it," Rosa says as she holds the curtain open for us. Rosa is a tiny woman, but I'm a tall one, so I duck a little as I go under the curtain.

I'm excited to be going back here, as it's rare for anyone to be invited into Rosa's kitchen. She hands me a hairnet to match hers before I'm allowed to step foot past the threshold, and I gladly put it on. She looks Pearl over with a second hairnet in her hands, apparently decides it isn't necessary, and puts it back. She then walks us through the kitchen where all the fantastic candy is made—a surprisingly normal-looking kitchen, no stereotypical witchy stuff here—and into the back office. We sit down on a simple, pink sofa and she sits on an office chair at the desk in front of us.

"So, tell me what happened."

"Well, I found a box under the brick floor at the baseball stadium. Please don't tell anyone I found it there because Brigley will try to take it."

"Your secret is safe with me," Rosa says as she makes the lip-zipping motion.

"Thank you. The box had the logo from this shop on it. Inside the box was a Ghostlight Falls women's baseball team baseball card from the forties with her," I point to Pearl, "on it. There isn't any record of a women's baseball team ever being here, though. There was also an empty gum wrapper, and a letter inside saying that whoever found the box was supposed to protect 'her.' It didn't say who *her* was, but I think we can assume it meant Pearl. The letter also said to beware of Brigley and was signed 'V.'

With the logo being from Rosa's and it being signed V, it made me think it was your grandma. Pearl had a dream that I think confirmed it."

"It does sound like it. Did you bring the letter?"

"Yes, duh, I should have given it to you." I shake my head at my own forgetfulness and hand it to her.

Rosa reads the letter, a smile appearing on her face as she does.

"This is my grandmother's handwriting. I know it's a serious message, but I can't help smiling. It's been a long time since I've seen any-thing new from her. What happened next?"

"Well, I just read the card and tried to figure out if it meant anything but couldn't. I left to get a drink of water, and when I came back, there was Pearl."

Rosa looks at me silently for a moment.

"Did you spill anything on the card? Did you say anything? Any spell words?"

"No, I didn't spill anything. I don't even know any spells."

"Did you say anything at all?"

My face heats to about a zillion degrees as I look briefly at Pearl and find her watching me intently. I look back at Rosa and swallow thickly.

"Um. I just said I wished I had a girlfriend that likes baseball as much as I do."

Pearl's face lights up.

Rosa nods. "That'll do it."

"What do you mean?" I ask.

She ignores me entirely and turns to Pearl. "Honey, what do you remember about how you got here?"

Pearl's gaze drops to her folded hands. "At first, I didn't remember anything. Then last night while I was sleeping it all came back to me."

She tells Rosa about Brigley, how he started off kind, then turned cruel. She then tells her everything she told me last night. Everything about the disappearing girls and Valentina hiding them. Even about accidentally swallowing her gum and hiding the fact. When she's done, Rosa sits quietly for a moment in thought, pink pen tapping her chin, before she speaks.

"Why was Brigley making the girls disappear?" she asks.

Pearl pauses for a moment to think. Just when it seems like she isn't going to remember, she gasps.

"He was mad that we were more popular than the Wonder Balls. He owned their team, but not the stadium, and he wanted both. The Wonder Belles all lived in Ghostlight Falls full-time, did tons of charity work, and we packed the stands every game. We were making so much money for the town, that they weren't in any hurry to put the Balls back in, or to kick us out. Don't get me wrong, everyone loved the Balls, and they would have been back in eventually, I'm sure! Things were just going real well for the Belles at the time and there was only one stadium." Pearl looks back and forth between Rosa and I, eyes pleading for understanding. "You get it, right? We weren't being selfish. We only wanted our chance to play."

I look her deep in the eyes and take both her hands. "Pearl, you really don't have to worry about that. You didn't do anything wrong. This is not your fault."

"Keep going, honey," Rosa says with a consoling nod.

Now more confident, Pearl continues.

"Brigley had closed his gum factory short-ly after returning from overseas and announced he was focusing entirely on baseball. He tried and tried to buy out the Belles, but we were self-owned and determined to stay that way. It wasn't what anyone else was doing at the time, but with the problems some of the ladies had with men, we knew we were better off keeping our money and power to ourselves. Besides, it was clear Brigley just wanted to shut us down and put his Balls back in. Well, rather than trying to figure out a way for both teams to play, or using diplomacy to get us out, I guess Brigley took a different route."

"What a piece of shit," Sharon says from a shadowy corner on the opposite side of the room. Pearl and I both startle, only now aware of the fact that she was lurking there.

"That's for sure," Rosa says, twirling her pink pen between her fingers. "Alright, let's break it down. Piece of Caca Brigley went to war, and either he was infected with some nasty crea-ture, or something else entirely came back pre-tending to be him. He started making women disappear. My beautiful grandmother, may her soul rest peacefully, saved some of them using a strange cobbled together spell I've never seen. Brigley erases all memory of the women's team from history. He gets everything he wants."

Rosa stands up and begins to pace back and forth in front of her desk, still twirling her pen. "Many decades later, Delia trips over a brick, finds one of the spelled boxes, wishes for love, and out comes Pearl. Unfortunately for Pearl, she is two-dimensional, probably because she did not spit out the gum like my grandmother told her to."

"It was an accident!" Pearl mumbles.

"Rules are rules!" Rosa says sternly, pen pointed at Pearl, before returning to her pacing. "According to Pearl, some of the women may still be hidden in boxes in the stadium. Is that everything?"

She stops and looks at the two of us. We nod.

"We'll have to get rid of Brigley—you know that, right? He's not going to let witnesses come back to out him." Rosa taps her pen on her chin again as it dawns on me that she means it *is* the Brigley I know. Not his grandpa. *Yikes*. She sighs. "It's unfortunate that it took this long to get you out, Pearl, but love is like that sometimes."

"Love?" Pearl says at the same time I say, "Get rid of Mr. Brigley?"

Though, to be honest, the love part is first on my mind too.

Rosa holds her hands up.

"I'll answer what I can. Brigley has been around since I was a child, and he looked the same then. As far as I know, he was the same before I was born. I don't know anything about what he was like before that."

"Then it must be the same Brigley from my time," Pearl says with a frown. "He's a real piece of work."

"I don't know what he is," Rosa says. "But he's not the normal human he pretends to be. That I've always known. Which is fine, of course. We accept all kinds here. But whatever he is makes the spirits nervous. I haven't bothered to find out what he is; what people are is normally none of my business. If we're going to get rid of him however, we first have to know what we're up against."

"I'll go to the bookstore," Sharon says. "The owner loves me. She always has piles of obscure shit waiting when I visit. Terrible for my wallet, great for research. Then I can hit up the library. The restricted section hates to see me coming."

How she can make every word, no matter how intriguing, sound just completely devoid of emotion, I have no idea. Used to drive me absolutely insane when we dated. I mean, she's a really cool person, she's just not—

I look over at Pearl, whose blue eyes are somehow glistening in the soft light. No, they're not *really* wet, but the emotion on her face is so strong they might as well be. Yet, even with all the stress she's under, she turns to me, squeezes my hand, and offers me a little smile to try to make *me* feel better about our situation.

Even with the shakiness in her voice I can tell she's trying to brighten my mood when she says, "It'll be alright. We'll get him, Delia. Whatever the heck he is."

Fuck, she's amazing. She returns her attention to the Candy Witch. Her hands are now folded in her lap as she leans toward Rosa. Her voice shakes slightly when she speaks, the fear evident.

"Can you fix me?" Pearl asks. I can see the shine of tears in her eyes; my heart breaks.

"I don't know." Rosa finally sets down her pen and taps a finger to her lips. "Delia, have you tried going inside of Pearl?"

Pearl and I look at each other with confused expressions before turning back to Rosa.

"I'm sorry, *inside of*? Like entering a building?" Pearl asks.

"As in, has Delia attempted to put any part of herself inside you?"

"What? No. She's flat." I say, words tumbling out of me quickly.

"Don't be so stuffy," Rosa scoffs. She waves Pearl toward her. "Here, I need to test something."

Pearl stands, looking nervously over at me, before looking back at Rosa.

"I have a feeling you're gonna stick your hand in my mouth, aren't you?" she says with a resigned sigh.

I cough. *What?*

"I'm going to try to, yes."

Pearl bends over the desk and Rosa does just that. To my surprise, when Rosa slides her fingers against Pearl's mouth, they disappear inside of it. It's like the police box ship in that sci-fi show from the U.K.—the one that's been on the air for decades.

She's bigger on the inside.

"Holy shit. How does that work?" I ask as I scramble to my feet, desperate for a closer look.

Pearl gags as Rosa pulls her hand out, something pink and stringy coming along with it. Whatever the pink stuff is continues to stretch out of her throat in a long rope, much like hot mozzarella cheese. She whines and gags as the strings wind out.

"Just a little more, sweetie," Rosa says softly to Pearl.

After several more seconds, the pull is complete, and a fat, sticky, pink blob rests on the desk before Rosa. Pearl coughs and strokes her throat.

"What was that?" she says on a rasp.

"Bubblegum. I assume it had the magic in it. Remember, you're supposed to spit gum out. This is a big problem." Rosa shakes her head.

"Don't you listen to what your parents tell you? *Don't swallow gum!*"

"I had terrible parents!" Pearl snaps grumpily as she sits back down. "And, again, it was an accident!"

Rosa shrugs.

"So, can you fix me?" Pearl asks again with just about the saddest puppy eyes anyone has ever had, and it takes everything I have not to scoop her up and squeeze her.

"I don't know. With how long you've been in the box, it may take a while—if I can even do it at all, considering I don't know the spell to begin with, and it's been messed up with the gum swallowing." Rosa settles heavily back in her chair and folds her hands on her lap. "I'm so sorry I can't be more optimistic."

"It's alright. I'd take harsh truth over pretty lies any day."

I stroke the top of her hand softly and send her a reassuring smile.

"We'll figure something out. Ghostlight Falls will accept you however you end up, and I'll teach you about modern stuff. I know it's probably not how you imagined your life being, but I'll help you make it the best it can be. I promise."

Pearl begins to cry, tears falling down her face. Her tears are odd. They do look at first like they'd be wet, but they stay flat, just pictures on her slightly glossy paper that disappear when they reach her edges. I wonder where they go. Another one of her mysteries.

She sniffles softly. "Thanks, Delia. Can we go now? I'm worn out."

"Yeah. I'm tired too." I turn to Rosa as we stand and shake her hand. "Thanks so much."

"I'll work on trying to get Pearl into her original shape and finding the other girls. Sharon will work on figuring out what Brigley is. If we can do anything else, let me know." Rosa walks us to the front door but stops us right before we exit. "And my grandmother was right; stay away from Brigley."

As we walk out, holding hands, we're mostly quiet. Too many things are weighing on our minds. The thing itching at the top of mine right now is that Rosa never answered Pearl's question about love.

Chapter Five

Pearl

Well, I might be made of paper forev- er, I've been removed from history, and I'm filled with bubblegum. That's certainly not great news. I do have Delia, which is wonder- ful. Really, really wonderful. I've also discovered Doritos.

"Another one, please," I say with my hand held out.

"Are you sure? I really think we should watch what happens when you eat before you keep going." Delia sits across the sofa from me, holding the bag tightly against her chest with a wary look.

Neither of us knows where the "tortilla chips" are going when I eat them or where they'll end up, but once we discovered I could put things inside me we had to try. Kind of frightening to think about too hard, really, but we just had to do it! And these little triangles? They're *so good*. I really don't care what happens to me once they're inside. After the terrible day I've had I could use something nice.

"Hand them over."

"Just one more. Then we wait." She hesitantly pulls another orange triangle out of the bag and passes it my way.

I press the chip to my paper lips, and it slides on in. I crunch the spicy delight against teeth that feel normal to me—even though I know they don't exist as far as the outside world is concerned—and swallow it down. This whole situation just gets weirder and weirder. I cross my legs and lean lazily against the chair back.

"Well, that's that. Now, you can teach me about this online shopping thing. How do we get to the online shops? Do you have a car?"

Delia's eyes sparkle as she covers her mouth; she's trying not to laugh at me. That means I've said something dumb...again. I sigh and wait for her to compose herself enough to answer.

"*Online* means on the computer. Sorry, I should have explained better. We're going to look at pictures to pick out some ideas for you. Then we'll take them to a place in town that can make them custom fit for you, since you can't wear regular clothes." Delia says.

We did try, too—putting me in regular clothes, that is. They not only fell off, but also weighed me down. It was quite the failure.

Delia takes her phone out of her pocket and swipes her thumb on it so that it lights up. Mavis hops onto her lap and begins to turn in circles. "Alright, so let's cover the basics of the Internet. At least enough so we can find you some fancy new gear. We'll just learn as we go, okay?"

"*Meow. Pbft,*" Mavis says as she settles into a loaf. She makes a sound that sounds like a cross between an asthmatic wheeze and a purr. It's a bit unsettling but Delia doesn't pay it any mind so it must be fine.

I lean in and watch as Delia taps a symbol at the bottom of the phone and the picture changes. Then she touches a black space at the top of it and a bunch of letters show up.

"Looks kind of like a typewriter," I say.

"Yep, exactly. It's the keyboard. I type what I want to find into the search bar of the browser—that's what I tapped a second ago—and it will search the Internet for relevant information. The Internet is, basically, a place where people can put almost anything they want and do almost whatever they want with it. It's a little hit or miss sometimes because it doesn't matter whether or not the information people give it is true. So, if I ask something you know, and it gives me a wrong answer, please tell me."

"Will do. But, I must say, they really shouldn't let people lie about things there. Someone should clean it up so it's only the truth, shouldn't they? It seems the responsible thing for the people who own the Internet to do. I don't get why people are lying anyway. Who would waste their time going on their device to type in lies on the off chance someone might ask them a question? There are better things to do, if I say so"

"Well, the thing is...," Delia stares into the distance for quite a few seconds before continuing on as if I hadn't said anything. "Okay, so we need clothes for you. I have a crazy idea. First, I need you to tell me what kinds of clothes you'd like to wear. Modern stuff or your time stuff?"

"Well, I know I should want to fit in with modern fashion, but I can't help missing my things."

"Perfect, I was hoping you'd say that. I'm awful at fashion stuff and just, I don't know, girly stuff for the most part. I did find this website that has faithful recreations of vintage clothing though after looking around. The clothing is photographed from all directions in high resolution. It's really pretty and I think you would look amazing in all of it."

She types in the name of the "site", and it opens up to an image of a woman who looks like she stepped straight out of the forties. I can feel my face positively glowing.

"So now you can sort of scroll through like this and click on things that interest you to see more about them, or you can go to this magnifying glass here and type in specific words to look for. If you find something you really, really like let me know and I'll save it."

I learn it quickly, though I have to use a pen-like thing called a "stylus" to use the phone, as it doesn't recognize my fingers. Apparently, it only reacts to skin, and other materials made specifically for it—not paper. Regardless, it doesn't take long for me to select a *ton* of things that I like. I'll have to whittle it down when I get wherever we're going.

When we get done, Delia shows me how to work something called a microwave. It's incredible. While she's on a call with her mom, I attempt to microwave an egg by myself. It goes very poorly. She told me not to put metal inside of the microwave, as it would cause a fire. She didn't tell me that *eggs* would explode.

I stand staring at the open microwave with egg splattered all over inside of it. *What does one use to clean the inside of a microwave? Regular soap and water? Can I get water on myself, or will that ruin me? Hmm.*

"Pbft."

Mavis stands on her hind legs, puts her front paws on the edge of the counter, and sniffs inside the messy appliance. After a few good sniffs of the eggy funk, those long, creepy legs shoot out.

"Yikes!" I jump back, giving the cant as much room as she needs to do whatever the heck she's about to do.

Mavis pushes herself up higher with her longer legs, steadies herself on a bottom drawer with her lowest legs, and manages to work her upper body inside the microwave. I don't really know how to feel as she slurps and munches away, wheezing happily. It's a bit foul, but also, I like to see ladies succeed.

"How's it going?" Delia shouts from the living room.

"Fine! I'm coming!" I shout back then scurry out of there, leaving Mavis to her dinner. Delia is lounging on her purple sofa. Seeing her triggers a smile in me like always. "So, are we going to get my new clothes tonight?"

"The place we need is closed for tonight, unfortunately. We'll go right away tomorrow though. Speaking of tomorrow, I'm supposed to work in the afternoon." Delia bites her lip while she's lost in thought for a moment. "I know I'm supposed to stay away from Brigley, but I do see him at work sometimes. I don't think I can call in if I don't want to draw attention to us. Or maybe that's just paranoia. I don't know."

"If you're willing to risk it, I'm okay with it. It's up to you." I cover my mouth as I yawn. "I think it's gonna be an early night for me."

"Me too. Sleep sucked last night." Delia rubs her lower back. She does that a lot. Poor thing.

"I insist you sleep in the bed with me tonight. It'll be more comfortable on your back. Plus, you don't want to be out here with Mavis after she was rubbing up in all that hot egg."

"Hot egg? How did Mavis—"

I wave my hand dismissively. "You'll have to excuse my lack of pajamas. I have to sleep in my underwear. Can't exactly rest in my uniform."

"I have *zero* problem with that," Delia says as she stands. "But we'll make sure to add some pretty jammies to your shopping list."

"Good. I could use a few fancy things after the day I've had. Can't help but admit I enjoy feminine attire when I'm out of uniform. It seems many ladies these days dress in a more manly fashion." I think back to some of the half-naked people prancing around town. "Or just wear their unmentionables outside."

"They're not wearing underwear, just a different style," Delia says with a laugh. "I've even got a few skimpy tops myself."

"Really?" My lips quirk up at the sides. "You'll have to model them for me. In private."

Right on cue, her face turns red. My grin is wide as I get to the bedroom, and I begin to undress. Delia looks everywhere but at me.

"Uh, I'm gonna go to the bathroom and get dressed," she says as she takes her bundle of clothes and zips out the door.

Hmph. Fine then.

I finish undressing, peel back the blanket, and crawl into bed. A few moments later, Delia walks in dressed in plaid shorts and a white t-shirt. She stands in the doorway, still and wide-eyed, just looking at me. I don't know what the big deal is. It's not like I'm in anything fancy. We always wore boring red panties under our uniforms for good luck, and I've got a bra on of course. My camisole is a silly thing us girls made with the Wonder Belles logo, but nothing exciting. I did take my hair down—maybe she thinks I look sloppy. I smooth my hair and the front of my camisole self-consciously.

"Are you coming to bed or not?" I ask, patting the mattress beside me.

"I—do you want me to sleep on the sofa? It's not a problem. You can have the bed." She bites her lip ring and runs her fingers through her hair once again. What a nervous thing she's turned out to be.

"Just get in."

She climbs into bed, pulls the covers over us, and lays flat, staring at the ceiling. I fold myself onto my side so I can give her a perfectly grumpy look.

When her eyes finally dart to the side and notice me, she turns her head my way. "What? Why are you giving me that look?"

"Relax and get some rest."

"Okay." She turns back to face the ceiling for a moment before quickly turning back to me. "It's just that you look really beautiful. When I saw you it made me feel like I was gonna throw up—but, like, in a good way."

"That's some kind of compliment." I raise an eyebrow.

"Fuck. I'm not usually this much of an id-iot." She rubs her face then turns on her side to face me. "I just got overwhelmed by the sight of you laying there, looking like my dream woman. I don't want you to feel uncomfortable with me in bed next to you when it's stupidly obvious I'm attracted to you. So, if you want me to move that's okay. No hard feelings."

I finally do what I've been wanting to do for a while now. Softly, I tug on Delia's lip ring. She groans in the most delicious way as I bring her closer to me.

When she's a few inches away I let go of her lip ring, run my fingers over her hair, and say, "Don't you dare leave this bed. You've got to get your head in the game, doll. I'm Pearl Goddamn Monroe and I only play with winners. You hear me?"

"Absolutely," she says in a voice dropped low with desire.

The nervousness that was in her eyes drains out, replaced by the hungry passion I'd hoped for.

Next thing I know, her lips are pressed against mine. They're soft, warm, and much more pliable than my paper ones. For a second, I'm disappointed that my mouth stays two-dimensional, but when Delia slips her tongue between my lips everything changes.

Hungry moans escape Delia as the remainder of the shy girl that was there before is washed away. A yelp leaps from my mouth to hers as she rolls us over, leaving me flat against the mattress and her pressed against me. Only, being completely flat against the bed isn't ideal for either of us.

Delia breaks the kiss, pushes herself up to her elbows, and looks down at me. We're both breathing heavily, hearts racing fast.

"So, this position sucks. Do you mind if I rearrange some things?" Delia asks.

I shake my head with a laugh. "Go ahead, doll. Just be quick about it."

Delia grins back at me as she grabs some pillows and lines them up underneath me to give my body some height. When it's done, she crawls over me again. Things are much better. I push her striped hair behind her ears when we're nose-to-nose. She closes her eyes and lets out a deep breath before kissing me again, soft at first, but deeper and hungrier every moment that passes. I wrap my arms around her and run my fingers over the back of her hair and neck.

She pauses and pulls back to look at me. "Take off your top."

"Yes ma'am." I comply quickly, tossing my bra and camisole to the side.

"Holy fuck," she whispers as she looks me over.

I moan when she runs her thumb over my hard nipple. It must feel flat to her, hard or not, I realize. This is all so odd. I run my hand over my paper chest. My original chest is far from flat, but I'll make do with what I have now. I think I'm doing well, judging by the look on Delia's face. She leans over me, eyes on mine, and slowly, firmly, drags her tongue over my nipple. I grab the back of her head and hold on as she continues to lick and rub the area. She has me panting and writhing. Next, she's kissing my neck, then whispering in my ear while sliding her thumbs along the waistband of my panties.

"Take these off."

"Is it—will things—" I start to say, worried about the logistics, before she cuts me off.

"Let's find out."

It's a bit awkward with my flat legs, but I manage to get the panties off. At first, when I'm laying there, it's only a frontal view of my body. Which is nice and all, but that means minimal access to certain *inner* areas. Delia rotates my pelvis using the pillows to give me some dimension, and turns my hips in an odd way, but when folded just right she gets a nice view of my—

"You have a gorgeous pussy," Delia purrs against my knee, then begins to kiss her way up my thigh.

"Really? You think so?" I pant. Every time she kisses closer to my center, I feel myself throbbing harder and harder. I just want her to fucking touch me there. I swear I'll scream if she doesn't do it soon.

"So, so fucking pretty."

She's so close I can feel her breath on the lips of my cunt. The warm metal of her lip ring brushes against me so softly it tickles. My hips jerk. Delia holds my thighs on either side to keep me still. Her lips press against my paper softly with gentle kisses. I sigh at just the barest hint of relief.

I close my eyes and send out a silent prayer to whatever gods are in charge of two-dimensional vaginas. *Please, please, give this woman the ability to fuck me.*

Her tongue slides smoothly along the valley between my thighs. An absolutely pathetic whimper escapes me as I feel her brush against my clit.

"*Mmm.* Still no paper cuts. We're getting somewhere," Delia says before licking me again, firmer, her tongue sliding deep between my folds, pressing hard against my clit.

"Yes, yes." Nothing more interesting to say comes out of me. Her eyes make it impossible to think of anything else.

Those beautiful eyes stay on mine as she slips two of her fingers inside me. As she curls them just right against my sensitive insides, and laps at my throbbing outsides, I wonder if waiting eighty years for this wasn't such a bad deal after all.

"You taste like bubblegum," Delia says with a grin as her fingers work inside me. Her tongue flicks over the ring on her lip. "Such a sweet girl."

"Sweet?" I say breathlessly as I writhe below her. "I'm a goddamn Wonder Belle."

I grab a fistful of her hair and push her face back between my legs. Her laugh vibrates against me as she goes back to licking enthusiastically. Very soon after, I'm shouting her name as I come. My back and feet arch so hard I think I may have permanent creases in my paper. I love every second of it.

"Oh my god, Delia, that was amazing. You're amazing. How was that even possible? My mind feels like—I can't even—" I pause as I watch her rise to her knees.

A concerned look overtakes Delia as she pulls stringy, stretchy, pink stuff from her face and hands. It's stuck on there pretty good and it's unfortunately clear what it is.

"We have another bubblegum situation."

"Did that—that didn't—" I scramble to sit up and try to get a look, but I'm in an awkward position on these pillows. "That didn't come from me, did it?"

"Yeah, it did. When you—you know—," Delia says with a cocky little grin, "came all over my face. Which was pretty fucking hot, by the way. Totally worth the clean-up, Bubbles."

"It's still embarrassing." *That better not become a nickname.* I run my hand between my legs to check for damage to my paper, but find myself clear of the sticky mess. "Oh, well that's good. It didn't stick to me. Seems strange that it wouldn't stick to paper of all things."

"Hmm. I'm assuming it's something magic related, but honestly, I don't understand that stuff." Delia takes some kind of moist cloth out of a crinkly package and begins to scrub at the gum on her face and hands.

"Same here. Ghostlight Falls was a lot smaller back in my time, and a lot more isolated. The only people that lived here needed to be here to hide or chose to be here because of who they are. Like me." I look around Delia's room as I carefully try to tug my underwear back on without ripping them. "Delia, why are you in Ghostlight Falls?"

"My family moved here when I was a baby. I like it here, so I don't plan on moving if I don't have to." She vigorously rubs the last bit of gum off of her fingers, tosses the cloth into her trash can, and pulls another out to work on her face some more. "I'm fully human, and so is my mom, but my dad's not. Well, he was. He got bitten by a weregorilla. He found out about this place and moved us here."

"Well, I'm glad he did. Moved you, that is. The gorilla bit is unfortunate."

"Weregorilla. Totally different." Delia laughs.

"My apologies."

"I think I'm ready for bed once I get this off, if you are. We have a lot to look forward to tomorrow." She tosses that wipe into the trash and grabs another one.

"I agree. I'm ready for the future."

Chapter Six

Delia

I called in sick. Thankfully, Brigley's part-time secretary took the message. That's a win for sure. Now I just have to creep around town and not get caught by the scary murderer. It's fine, I'm not freaking out at all. Except when I am. I'm hiding it though, for Pearl's sake.

After we woke up, got ready, had a quick breakfast—we've figured out Pearl doesn't need to eat, but she sure likes snacking—and cleaned out a mysteriously furry microwave, we set out into town for Sheet-y Stationary.

The problem is the store doesn't stay put. The building has a tendency to get up and go at any moment. So, we need to ask the town map. We head to the visitors' center so I can find Mappy and ask him. Mappy has the location of every place in town on his body, and it updates in real time. Wherever Sheet-y is, he'll know.

As suspected, when we turn the corner, he's standing out front in his little booty shorts, flexing his muscles for all the passersby. I sigh and shake my head as I approach him. You gotta love the town himbo.

"Heya, Mappy. I'm looking for Sheet-y. Any help?"

He raises an eyebrow and inspects his nails. I cross my arms over my chest. We always do this.

"What's in it for me?" he asks as he shifts back on his bare feet.

"The joy of friendship," I reply with a marked lack of enthusiasm.

Mappy leans forward and pinches my cheek.

"Such a charmer." He notices Pearl standing behind me and winks at her. "I do love athletic women."

"She's taken, my guy," I say firmly, as I poke Mappy in the chest.

Okay. I didn't mean to say she's taken. Because, I mean, she's not officially. Right? Fuck.

Whatever. Plus, Mappy isn't serious with his flirting anyway. *Chill, Delia.*

Pearl giggles and Mappy grins.

"Oh, I like that. Maybe we'll get to see you out and about more, Delia. Would be nice." He gently punches me on the shoulder and the smile he gives me is one of genuine happiness. He *is* my friend, after all. Of course he's happy I've got a girlfriend.

I mean, if she is my girlfriend, that is.

Mappy stands back and stretches his arms. The muscular man unfurls two massive bat-like wings, revealing the rest of the town's map. He looks over both of them carefully before nodding at the left one.

"Over by Ratcliffe's. Looks like it's blocking the center of the Dreadweather Forest bike path. People are gonna be mad about that." He shakes his head and curls his wings back against his body.

"Better than the time it landed in the middle of the baseball stadium." I laugh. Brigley was *pissed* about that.

"Much better." Mappy laughs.

"Alright." I turn to Pearl. "Let's get going before the store moves again. Catch ya later, Mappy!"

We walk toward the store, getting to know one another a little better while I explain things we see that weren't around in 1946. Which is a whole lot. Even when I used the phrase "catch ya later" with Mappy, that was new to her, I guess, but she likes that one—says it reminds her of baseball.

When we pass by a Pride flag in a shop window, I tell her about some things that have changed for queer folks in the country, and the world—progress we've made, things we're still fighting for—and she has to take a seat on a park bench to process her thoughts.

We sit in front of the Dreadweather Forest, even though it's not a great idea to sit on the benches on a hot day, especially wearing a tank top. Everyone knows not to because of the giants and their...*habits*. It seems like she's not really thinking about giants right now, so I'll take the risk for her—even though I'm wearing my shoulder-baring tank top with the spadefoot toad-print fabric I got at the Spadefoot Toad Museum's iconic gift shop.

"So, two women can really get married legally *outside* of Ghostlight Falls now?" Pearl asks, her eyebrows pinched as she waits for my answer.

"Yep, in a bunch of countries, at least. Not everywhere, unfortunately. Here though, yeah." I pull out my phone and search up a video from a while back. "Watch this. It's not very long but it's the speech the president gave when they legalized same-sex marriage."

Pearl takes the phone in shaking hands and watches with wide eyes. Not very long into the speech she begins to cry and she's fully sobbing by the end of it.

"That was our President? And he said that? I want to know more about history. Not just for us. For everyone. What else happened?" She starts to poke at the screen, but I gently take the phone away.

"Later. There's so, so much. Let's get to Sheet-y first. Is that cool with you?" I stand up and hold my hand out...

...but can't reach her before something huge grabs me around the waist.

A giant hand wraps around me before I can even register that an arm has burst out of the forest. The buckles on my boots jingle rapidly as I'm tugged toward the tree line. *Oh no.* I know what's coming and I'm not happy about it.

"God damn it, you stinking giant! Go to rehab!" I shout right before the tip of a huge, wet tongue pokes out between two pines. "Aww, hell."

Sluurrrp. The forest giant licks from my lower back all the way up to my hair line. *Blech.* Sticky slobber residue coats my skin and the entire backside of my top.

"Gross! You messed up my toad tank top!" I yell.

Not that it matters what I say. The forest giants don't care. They rarely interact with anyone other than licking us to get high. Humans are to them like some toads are to people; lick our backs, get fucked up. They *really* like it, and it's *super* addictive, but that's about all they've told anyone.

The giant sets me down and slinks back to where he came from.

"That's right! You go home; you jerk!" I pull some foliage off a bush and start wiping as much of the gunk off of me as I can. *Yuck.*

"Well, some things don't change, I guess. Darn giants," Pearl says as she takes my hand and begins to walk again. "It is a nice top. Even if it's a bit scandalous."

"Scandalous? You should see what's under it." I tug her forward as I spot the entrance to the stationary store.

"I look forward to it, doll."

My grin is about ten feet wide when I push open the door to Sheet-y. The place is a wreck, loose paper flung everywhere, boxes tipped on their sides, signage lopsided. It's clear that the store must have picked itself up and walked here not long ago.

"Tillie! Are you around?" I shout toward the back room.

"Coming!" a woman yells back, right before the sound of a cardboard box avalanche. "One more sec!"

Pearl looks at me questioningly but I just shrug. Tillie's a bit of a whirlwind. The two of us look at cards and fancy paper for a couple of minutes until she comes out, hair flying out wildly from a messy bun, t-shirt covered in dust.

"How can I help you?" Tillie asks breathlessly.

"I'm wondering if you could print me something on the *big* printer, please." I pull up the images on my phone as Tillie leans over the counter to look. "I need these to fit Pearl. Meet Pearl, by the way."

I point at an enthusiastically waving Pearl.

"Hi, Pearl. You're, um, flat? Right? Just asking because I'm gonna need measurements and I want to make sure I'm not losing my mind," Tillie says as she rubs her eyes. "Or maybe it was getting hit in the head by those boxes. Again."

"Oh, I'm flat, yes. Made of paper. Don't worry about your head."

"Well, paper I'm used to. Let's get going then," Tillie says with a smile as she pulls a toad-shaped tape measure from a drawer.

About an hour later Tillie walks out from the back room where she's been altering images, printing them, then fitting them to Pearl, in order to make a new paper wardrobe. Hopefully it's worked. They've refused to let me see during the process. Tillie clears her throat and says:

"Please welcome our very own movie star and baseball bombshell, Pearl Monroe." She steps aside then out comes Pearl.

My heart skips a beat when I see her there, laughing and doing exaggerated modeling poses, as if this isn't serious. As if I haven't just realized I've got it *bad* for a hundred-something-year-old cursed lady who's made of paper, filled with bubblegum, and who my evil boss wants to erase from existence. When I see her smiling in that blue fit and flare shirtwaist dress, with its red poppy pattern matching the adorable red shoes they even managed to craft, it somehow makes everything finally feel *real*. She's not a baseball card; she's *Pearl Monroe*. And I want her to be mine.

Chapter Seven

Pearl

I don't really get how it works, but it does. Tillie made them out of paper, fitted them to me, and they went from stiff to moving fine—as long as I'm the one doing the moving, of course. That's some kind of magic Valentina had!

I'm glad now because I've got a whole new wardrobe. Delia offered to carry the folder of clothes back home for us, but it's several feet tall and quite heavy, so that was unrealistic. She used her phone to request a driver to come get us instead. Paid the fee with the phone and everything! I swear, next she'll tell me the damn thing has buttons to bring her food too.

Delia drags the heavy folder into her room and leans it against her closet. She runs her fingers through her sweaty hair before asking me a question.

"So, are you gonna show me the rest of them? I didn't get to see everything at the store."

"Where's the fun in that? You can see them as I wear them each day."

"Boo," she lowers one thumb at me, "No fun. I'm gonna take a shower. Get the giant slime and sweat off of me. You're lucky you don't have to deal with this."

Delia digs through her drawers until she finds what she wants, then heads off to the bathroom. When I hear the water running, I turn on her phone with the stylus, pull up the history site she showed me, and start to read from 1947. She's not in the shower long, so I don't get far, but I'm determined to continue every chance I get. When Delia comes into the room, however, there's no way I'll be able to retain any information. Not with how she looks right now.

Delia's wearing a men's undershirt, one of the thin, sleeveless, white ones. There's something odd about how her nipples look under it. I don't want to be rude by asking about it, but the shirt is quite revealing. It's making me quite curious.

"You're staring at my tits. It's getting weird," Delia says, interrupting my internal debate.

"What if I am? You're the one walking around here like some kind of floozy," I toss my hair behind my shoulders and inspect my nails.

Delia stares at me silently for a moment before tossing the towel into a basket across the room. "A floozy? Hmm. That's definitely a new one for me."

"If it fits, it fits. You're practically offering your bosom on display."

Delia rolls her eyes at me and my attempt at a serious expression fails. I smile at her as she grabs her hairbrush and crawls onto the bed, relaxing with her back against the pillows and brushing her wet hair back out of her face.

With all that hair out of the way, I can see all her face at once; she's gorgeous. She has high, angular cheekbones, full lips, hooded eyes, and a slightly crooked nose that she must have broken at some point. The nostril piercing, lip ring, and fun hair distracted me before so much that I didn't notice she has a little tattoo on the side of her *neck.* Well, it's by her ear. A little, cracked and bent baseball bat. Her eyes dart to mine again and when she sees me watching her, she drops the brush with a sigh.

"What?"

"Nothing. I just really like looking at you a whole lot," I say softly as I sit down next to her. "And I'm looking forward to kissing you some more."

"I'd like that too." Her eyelids grow heavy as she begins to fold the edge of my skirt upward. "And I'd like to see if you printed off any of the more intimate items I picked out."

I gently slap her hand away, giving her a reproachful look as I do so.

"Don't curl the edges, you'll ruin it. Let me do it."

Delia watches with a fire that could turn my edges to ash as I stand in front of her carefully undoing each of the buttons holding my dress together. When it comes apart, I set the pieces on the chair next to me and pose for my sweetheart. The pale blue slip is so short it barely covers my goodies. It's satiny and trimmed in bubblegum pink lace. I've got a matching pink garter holding up my stockings and when I move, I'm sure she can catch a glimpse of the pink panties I've got on. I swish my hips back and forth a little to make sure she can.

"Damn, I'm good at picking out clothes," she says with a smirk as she leans back on her hands. "Come here, Bubbles"

Giggling at the damn nickname, I hop onto the bed and settle lightly onto Delia's lap, one leg on each side of hers. She lifts the hem of my slip and peeks underneath, raises an eyebrow, and makes an approving sound.

"Hey," I say with a laugh. "Might as well just take it off.

She shrugs. "Might as well."

A sigh breaks free from my lips as Delia begins to kiss my neck. The throbbing it immediately causes between my legs has me scrambling to unlace the side of my slip. Shortly after I'm sliding it onto the floor and Delia's moved to kissing my lips. I run my hands over her smooth hair and the sides of her face. She breaks the kiss and pulls back to look me over.

When she takes in my pink lingerie, she grins. "Yep, I'm good at shopping for you."

"Let me see you," I say as I tug at the edges of her shirt.

"Okay," she says. She kisses the tip of my nose and looks me straight in the eyes. "Don't be weird."

"What do you mean?" I ask. Of course, I wouldn't be anything but kind to her.

"Just—" She sighs. "Let's just take things as we go. I'll tell you if I'm not comfortable with something. Okay?"

"Of course." I stroke her cheek. "Always."

Delia kisses me softly before lifting her shirt over her head. I lean back and my eyes widen as I see my beautiful darling in front of me. The first thing that catches my eye are the pieces of metal going through her nipples. I certainly didn't expect that, but it's not unpleasant. I'll come back to those.

I don't mention the scars across and down her center, but I can't stop myself from reaching out and touching one. I drag my finger all the way along the white line from the edge of her shorts to her bellybutton.

"Accident," she says softly. "When I was a kid. Same reason my back's all messed up."

I gently tug on the little barbell in her nipple and raise a questioning brow. Delia hisses and grabs my hand.

"Not from the accident. Fully intentional," she says with a laugh.

"Did that hurt?"

"Not one bit."

I tug, a bit harder this time, on the other piercing. Delia bites her lip and groans.

"Fuck, Pearl. I'm sensitive. Be careful."

"Careful? Like this?" I ask as I tug both piercings at once, leaning in to kiss her as I do.

Delia moans into my mouth as I rub, pull, and tease her nipples. I've never been with a woman who was this sensitive in that area, and I have to admit I find it exciting. She writhes under my hands and for the first time since I've been revived, I feel like I have some kind of control. Soon enough though she stops my hands and breaks our kiss.

The look in her eyes is desperate as she says, "I need to fuck you. Now."

She begins to move as if to lift me from her lap but stops.

A look of concern dulls the fire in her eyes as she asks, "Wait, they had—never mind, of course they did. One sec."

She gets up then, heads to her closet, and pulls out a black bag. It has straps and looks like something one would carry to the woods or in the army.

"My bag of tricks," she says with a wink as she rifles through it. "Set up your pillows, Bubbles."

I can't help but wiggle with excitement as I set the pillows up like they were last time, then lay on top of them.

"Lay on your belly this time, beautiful," she says, voice husky. *Oh, my goodness.*

"Well, yes ma'am."

I follow her instructions, even though I feel a little silly. It's hard not to feel self-conscious like this. Not sure how she can find me attractive when I'm just flopped over like a pancake.

"You look so fucking good, Pearl," Delia says as the mattress creaks under her weight, closer and closer. "Let me take these off and see your sweet pussy."

"Please do whatever you like."

Delia very, very slowly removes the pink underwear, humming in delight as she does. She casts them to the side and spreads my legs apart.

"Such a nice view. I could get used to this," she practically purrs as she slides her hands along my thighs. One hand continues up until she meets my soft center and she gently inserts a finger inside me. "I took out the toys, Pearl, to fuck you with. I'm wearing one now. Is that alright?"

She inserts two more fingers, beginning to stretch me, moving fluidly, slowly.

"Yes, it's alright. I've—I've done things before."

"Okay. Good. I want to make sure you're always comfortable."

Delia slips her fingers out of me, unfortunately, though she kisses my rump in apology when I whine. I can't see behind me very well in my state, so I just have to trust her, I guess.

The tip of something cool and firm touches my entrance all of sudden and I tighten up in surprise for a second.

"I'll take it slow," Delia says reassuringly as she rubs it along my folded entrance. "Are you ready?"

"Yes. I want it," I breathe out. "Please."

Delia presses her body against mine, licks along the back of my neck, and whispers, "Then let's get you nice and sticky."

Chapter Eight

Delia

*F**uck, it's been a long time since I've done this. Come on Delia, you got this.*

Pearl is draped over the pillows underneath me facedown, partially because I fucking love an ass-up view, and partially because I didn't want her to see what a nervous wreck I am. This may be a weird as hell situation, but she's still a beautiful woman, in my bed, waiting for me to give her a good time. So, I better bring it.

I aim the long-neglected equipment to her paper cunt and hope for the best. How this is going to fit, I don't know, but I just have to hope it will. Thankfully, I chose a reasonable size today, and somehow the magic lets her stretch around it. I press forward, and inch by inch the silicone disappears like magic.

Pearl moans and whimpers maddeningly beneath me. When I'm all the way inside of her, I work my hips languidly in and out, getting used to the strap again. I lean over her and whisper in her ear, "You're the hottest thing I've ever heard. I could listen to you moan all night. All day."

"It feels so good. Oh, Delia."

I grip her ass as I thrust in and out firm enough to crumple it but not enough to damage her. "You've got a perfect little ass too, did you know that?"

She moans as she pushes her ass against me, "Go harder, faster."

I huff out a soft laugh. "Anything for Pearl Monroe."

I work up to a faster rhythm before forcing myself as hard as I can into her without risking any...*tearing.* When she's groaning deeply in pleasure, I decide it's the time to kick it up a notch. With a devious grin I reach down and click the switch.

"Oh, yikes!" Pearl yelps as the vibrating starts.

"Hold on tight, Bubbles," I say between ragged breaths, "Enjoy the ride."

Pearl comes in less than a minute, sticky pink bubblegum coating my boxer briefs...and I haven't even gone past the lowest setting. Her excitement is also turning *me* on like crazy. Combined with the secondhand vibration, I'm feeling something brewing in myself. Which is...unusual.

Now, I'm *very* much a giver. I don't like receiving—at all. It's just not my thing, and it won't be. I can still have an orgasm, just not through someone else's touch. For it to even happen this way with someone normally takes time, and trust; never a first encounter. It happening now with Pearl? Well, I'm not mad.

"What the hell is that? Pearl asks, sounding nearly crazed as she tries to pull away from the sensation.

I tug her against me as I continue fucking her, turning the setting up higher. I know they had vibrators back in her day, but not ones like *this*. She shakes below me, the sounds coming out of her throat are desperate and wild. I can feel the pressure building between my legs. My movements begin to falter, my rhythm less steady.

"Give me another one, Pearl," I grind out between my teeth.

With my name screamed into the pillow she does, more gum coating me. *Fuck this is gonna be hard to clean up.*

"Fuck, Delia, I love you," she shouts.

And *that* breaks me. I come as I fuck my paper doll, my perfect pitcher, the woman I've searched for forever. I don't know if she meant it or not, but it's true that *I* feel it. *I fucking love her.*

"Pearl, fuck, yes," I mumble out a bunch of one syllable bullshit when I should be spouting poetry. I'm too busy thinking with my pulsing clit at the moment for sonnets, however.

My thighs shake as I grow slippery in the fabric between them. I really love Pearl. She's so amazing. Everything is amazing.

Oh my god, my brain is mush.

I fumble for the switch and turn off the vibrator, grab the pillows, and roll the whole bundle of us over, then shove the pillows away, so it's just Pearl and I spooning. There's gum everywhere, but it can wait.

"I've made a mess," she says softly.

"I don't care. I'll buy new sheets."

"You'll buy new sheets every time we have sex? That doesn't sound practical."

"That sounds to me like you plan on staying around a while. I'll do what I gotta do to keep you if that's true."

She shuffles sideways and I help her turn around to face me. It's so strange to watch her kinda disappear for a second when she turns to the side. I don't like that one bit. I'm happy when she's facing me again, her cheeks flushed from making love, and the biggest smile on her face.

"I do like it here so far. It hasn't been long, of course, but I've already got a whole new wardrobe, some education, good sex, and most importantly, Doritos." Pearl kisses my nose to punctuate her sentence.

I offer her a frown. "Tortilla chips are the most important?"

"Only slightly more important than all the sex."

"I'll have to work on improving my rank then."

Pearl rubs her hips against mine where the strap is still attached. "I guess you will."

The clean-up sucked. I did, in fact, throw my sheets away. I have another set, and I'll buy another one tonight online, but we're gonna have to figure something else out. Despite my earlier words, I do not have infinite bedding money. I'll try to find something that we can wipe off. Plastic or vinyl maybe. *Ugh*, that sounds like sensory hell. Worth it for her. My room smells good though. I love the smell of bubblegum.

I had the dreaded talk with Pearl about how I'm strictly giving, no receiving. This has been a...*rough* moment for me in more than a couple relationships. A lot of people are super shitty or just think they can "fix" me, when there isn't anything to fix. But Pearl? Of course, everything was perfect. She was really cool about it, which was a major relief. Pearl says she's fine with the fact that I love making her come, and if that's all I need to make me happy then she's not complaining. Plus, she still gets to play with my tits, and I guess she likes that. More power to her. Play away, Bubbles.

We sit around and watch movies that are about her time period, and she makes a game of pointing out inaccuracies. Mavis plays nice and even sits on top of Pearl without scratching her. We eventually stop the game when she gets angry at a superhero film because the superhero gets way too much credit for killing the bad guys in a real life war. I guess I can understand why that would tick her off.

We shuffle off to bed and lay in the dark quietly for a while before Pearl speaks up.

"We're going to save the girls, right?"

"We gotta handle Brigley first. But yeah, we're gonna try."

It's quiet again until I can hear Pearl softly snoring. My stomach hurts as I think about how we're going to get the other girls out. I enjoyed this free day of doing nothing but now we have to do the right thing. And I'm scared.

I don't get much sleep.

The next morning, Pearl shakes me awake with, "Hey doll, I was reading history on your phone, and a little rectangle popped up. It said 'Sharon' on the top and 'Come to the store' underneath that."

We head to Rosa's first thing. Sharon waves us to the back as soon as we walk in and hands me a hairnet as I pass by. Rosa is at her desk, drinking a coffee, and reading from what's possibly the thickest book I've ever seen.

"Sit, sit," she waves to Pearl and me as we take our seats. "We've figured him out. Now's the time to plan, ladies."

"We're ready to hear what you found," I say as I take Pearl's hand in mine.

Sharon closes the door behind her, leans against it, and crosses her black velvet-wrapped arms across her chest. "I looked up his military records, since we know that whatever changed him happened when he was deployed. He was sent to Italy, but when the battle was won, he didn't return with the rest of the troops. They didn't find him until 1945, and when they did, he was on some island in Greece. I had to dig pretty deep to find the rest, but apparently, when they found him, he was alone in a dark room. It was filled with shallow water and la-beled 'Experiment: Reminisce.' Fucked up stuff. There wasn't much else I could find, but mom and I started putting the pieces together."

Rosa jumps right into where Sharon left off, eyes sparkling with excitement. "Now, you must understand that this is all a guess, but we're pretty confident. It's going to sound a little crazy. Just listen though."

"I'm made of paper. Crazy is my life," Pearl shrugs.

Rosa points at Pearl. "Crazy is this whole damn town. Anyway, we need to send him to the underworld."

"You want to send him to *hell*?" Pearl interrupts, her hand on her chest, her eyes wide with shock. "I don't think I can do that, even to someone so terrible."

"Oh, sweetheart, there are many different worlds. When I say underworld in this case, I'm referring to somewhere not for you and me. Somehow, Sharon and I think the monsters—*human* monsters—who captured Brigley brought water from Hades, the Greek underworld, to ours."

Rosa glances at Sharon, who nods at her to continue.

"They used it to do something to him—something that changed him into a creature that's no longer human and no longer meant for," Rosa spreads her hands out wide, then raises them up, "this place."

"I looked up how to send a baseball coach, who's been possessed by water from the river Lethe, back to Hades, before he can poof a paper woman out of existence. Obviously, that led me nowhere," Sharon says, dryly as always. "I did look more into the river itself and found that in some of the stories people can reverse the memory loss effects with water from the pool of Mnemosyne, which is also found in the underworld. I think if we're going to get rid of this guy, that'll be a major part of how."

"Oh, cool, so we just waltz into Hades and grab some water. No biggie." I groan as I flop backward on the sofa.

"So little faith." Rosa *tsks* me.

"Obviously I wouldn't bring it up if I didn't already have it," Sharon says as she unzips a pocket in her black skirt. She pulls out a purple vial with a wax seal top and waves it side to side. "I've got connections."

Pearl claps (though it doesn't make much sound) and giggles with glee. She asks, "Was it from the phone?"

Sharon shakes her head while Rosa snorts a laugh. I sit back up, heart racing with excitement now that I know we're close again.

"That's so awesome Sharon! What now?" I ask.

"Well, after we got this, we had to figure out what to do with it. We didn't know if he was able to be harmed in any traditional way, considering he's been alive so long. So, we had to test it."

"Oh, boy. You had to hurt him?" Pearl asks. "Who did you get to do that?"

"Angelo," Rosa replies. "He was at practice and was able to get close enough to scratch him with a hidden razor. Unfortunately, it didn't hurt him."

I slump in my seat. "Well, shit. He's invincible? How are we going to get to him?"

"We're gonna make him eat it," Sharon says.

"What? How?" I ask. "I never see him eat anything."

Rosa sighs, exasperated, with her hand on her forehead. "You do. All the time."

I think of Brigley's creepy face, trying to remember any time I've seen him eating, but all I can see is him either smoking a cigar or chewing—

"Oh! Gum!"

Rosa snaps her fingers "Now you're thinking! We're going to make the gum and give some to you and some to Angelo. Both of you will have some when you go to the stadium so whichever of you sees him first can offer it to him. We're also going to make something for you to locate the other girls, which should be much easier. I've made location spells before."

"Ah, this is so exciting! We're gonna save the girls!" Pearls says with the biggest grin.

"Come on, you can even watch me make it," Rosa says as she stands.

"Mom. Are you sure?" Sharon says, and for the first time in a long time I hear some actual emotion in her voice. She sounds...*annoyed.* "We don't let people watch us."

"Don't be jealous, mija. They're part of this now. It'll be fun."

"I'm not jealous." Sharon pouts in a way that says she definitely is jealous.

"Come on, everyone put on a white coat and gloves, and make sure your hairnet is secure. I like a clean kitchen." Rosa looks Pearl up and down. "If you have to touch anything I'll draw you some gloves or something. Just try not to."

Rosa sets bowls, utensils, and measuring cups on the stainless-steel counter. Sharon pours the contents of the vial into one of the smaller cups, then helps her mom get the rest of the ingredients.

"We're making the gum first," Rosa says as she sets down a jar of food coloring. "It's going to be mostly regular bubblegum ingredients, but I'll be adding the river water, pomegranate, oleander, and fine dust of broken mirror glass. The magic to make it all work, however, is up to us."

As soon as Rosa has all the ingredients prepared and takes the giant pot from its shelf, Sharon lets out an annoyed sigh. Then, both of their appearances begin to change. Pearl and I glance at each other, eyes wide, as the two of them transform into something neither of us would have ever expected.

"I—what? Why don't you tell anyone about this?" I ask Sharon.

She blows a glittering pastel curl out of her eyes as she picks up a spoon. Rosa laughs, sparkles filling the room that Sharon waves away with her baby blue satin gloved hand.

"No one needs to know. It's family business, okay? Promise you won't tell anyone."

Pearl and I both cross our hearts at the same time and in unison say, "I promise."

So, I guess I won't be telling anyone about Sharon and Rosa's story, but watching them make the candy was awesome, and I feel privileged to get the information I did.

Chapter Nine

Pearl

"*M eow. Pbft.*"

Mavis is hungry, again, so we feed her. It's about time to start getting ready for bed. Things took a long time at Rosa's, which I feel bad about considering she had to stay closed most of the day to help us. Then we did actual chores for Delia, like groceries and laundry and stuff, because I wanted to learn how things are done these days. It tired me out pretty early.

"Meow." Mavis rubs against my leg before heading to her bowl to eat. Ever since the egg incident she's been incredibly friendly.

"I'm gonna clean myself up, then I'm gonna put on a movie I think. I put the super magic gum in the fridge, so it doesn't accidentally melt or something. Also, so Mavis can't get at it," Delia says as she heads out of the kitchen.

"Sounds good to me."

As soon as she leaves, I open said refrigerator, snag a piece of turkey meat, and hand it to Mavis. The cant gobbles it up greedily, butts my leg with her head, then returns to her normal food as she makes that strange wheeze-purr sound. I pat her head and exit the kitchen.

As I'm walking through the living room, about to pass the front door, there's a knock. It's strange, considering the hour, and that Delia told me she rarely has visitors. Generally, I would consider it rude to answer someone else's door; however, I can hear that Delia is currently in the shower. This would be one of those times it would be appropriate to answer, I would think. As I'm debating, there's a second knock. Oh, heck. I'll do it. It's a nice town, who here could cause any trouble?

Smiling brightly, I pull open the heavy door—which is much more difficult than I'd anticipated, with my weight being so unfortunately low—and freeze. It seems there is one person who can cause trouble after all.

"You gonna invite me in, or what?" Mr. Brigley asks. He puffs his cigar, a cloud of smoke floating into the room.

"Uh, Delia doesn't allow smoking inside," I squeeze out. *Gotta buy time somehow.*

"Oh, well, if the hostess insists," he says in a mocking tone as he drops the cigar to the hall floor and grinds it out with his shiny, brown shoe.

Brigley pushes past me, crumpling my shoulder and nearly knocking me over. He plops his massive body down onto Delia's sofa and stares at me as I shut the door. All the shadows in the room seem to lean into him as if he were some kind of magnet for them. His mustache twitches and he sniffs.

"Sit, Pearl. Can you sit? I don't know what you can do when you're—what the hell are you? Cardboard? Fucking Christ. Just sit down."

I scramble to sit in the chair across from him. Anything to keep him from making me poof before we can find a way to get him to eat the gum. If we can.

"Where are the other girls?" he asks. *Right to the point, I guess.*

"Are you going to kill them?" I stammer out. *My turn to get to the point.*

"Yes. Now, where are they?"

"At least you're honest." I huff out a laugh filled with no joy. "Why would I tell you if you're going to kill them?"

"Because if you don't, I'll kill Delia."

"What's to say you won't kill her, and me, once I tell you anyway?" *Come on, Delia. We gotta get this guy.*

"Guess you gotta trust me. What other choice do you got?" He looks around the room. "Don't see anyone who can stop me from snapping my fingers and taking out whoever the fuck I want. All you people are lucky to still be here. Everyone in this goddamn town is only here because I haven't wiped them from existence. So, you're gonna do what I say, Pearl, or your girly goes bye-bye."

"I'll tell you." Delia stands in the opposite doorway, in her pajamas, water dripping from her hair. "Just warning you that we haven't found them yet, so I don't know what kind of condition they're in. We just got the magic to locate them today."

Brigley slaps his muscular thighs and smiles at me. "See, doll? That wasn't hard. Let's get this over with."

Brigley stands as Delia shoots me the briefest of glances. In that short glance, however, I see one sentiment: *I've got this.*

"It's in here. It's from the candy store. You've gotta chew it." Delia waves Brigley toward the kitchen as she starts to head there.

"That fucking family is nothing but trouble," Brigley mumbles as he follows Delia.

I hop up and follow them. The small kitchen feels cramped with all three of us in it. Delia stands awkwardly in front of the refrigerator, flexing and unflexing her hands and feet. Brigley stands stone still watching her.

"Get to it, Rogers," he barks.

"Okay, okay," she says as she opens the door and points to the lone piece of gum on the shelf. "You just chew it, and you'll know which direction to go to find them. Easy."

"Very easy." Brigley turns to me. My stomach drops. He sets his massive hands on my shoulders and crumples them in the process. I wince in pain. "Now, you chew it, and I'll follow you."

"What? Why me?"

"They're your teammates. Besides, I don't trust you two for shit. This way, I know it's safe." He pushes my shoulders harder. There's an awful sound as a piece of my neck tears. I can't hold back my scream and the pain shoots through me.

"Stop hurting her! We'll do what you want, just stop!" Delia screams, pulling at his arms.

Brigley lets me go. I slump forward and watch the wobble of the rubbery, pink strand slowly leaking from the crevice between my neck and shoulder, before standing upright again.

"*Merrrg*," Mavis says, an angry sound I didn't know she could make.

I look down and see her, fifth and sixth legs out, standing protectively over her food dish. It seems she doesn't like the perceived threat to her dinner. *Me either, buddy.*

"What the fuck is that thing?" Brigley asks.

"It's a cant. And she's wonderful," I reply. "Anyway, I'll chew the gum. No worries."

Delia looks at me with terror in her eyes. "I can do it, Pearl. It's okay."

"Nope, I've got it. It'll be fun," I say in the cheeriest tone I can work up as I open the door. I grab what I need from inside the refrigerator. "Hey, Mr. Brigley. Did you see the claws on Mavis's extra legs? If you look closely, they, uh, look like baseball gloves."

"They what?" Brigley crouches close to Mavis, squinting at her spider-like legs, as I wrap the piece of turkey against the side of the gum.

"Yeah, they're so strange. Hey, what did the baseball glove say to the ball?" I wave the turkey-covered gum just to the side of Brigley's face, but a little behind, so Mavis can see it and he can't. Her eyes widen at the sight of it.

Brigley turns to me, mouth open, ready to snap his cap at me for making a joke. Then I do what's just about the most cockeyed thing a dame could do. I lunge forward, and I cram the gum past *his* gums.

For a split second he's too shocked at my moxie to do anything, the turkey-wrapped piece of bubblegum half in, half out of his mouth as he crouches in front of Mavis. He doesn't take long to react, though. As Brigley slowly stands, I hear the "*hehhpppff*" sound of him beginning to spit the gum out—but not before Mavis does as I'd hoped she'd do.

The cant locks her eyes on the turkey, springs upward on her extra legs, and grabs at it. The man pulls back, reflexively sucking the gum back into his mouth in surprise. His teeth close on it, just once. That's all it takes.

Brigley freezes in place and the change begins immediately. His size rapidly decreases, all his strong muscles wither away, his back becoming hunched. His hair falls out and turns grey, until it's nothing but a few white, wispy strands. Brown teeth clatter to the floor. His skin becomes nearly transparent where it isn't spotted and splotched. Joints turn twisted and swollen. His eyes become cloudy, and they no longer have the frightening look they did. Eventually, he falls to the tile in a fetal position, wheezing but alive. The only other sound while Delia and I hold each other for the next few minutes is Mavis licking at her paws, until I finally speak up.

"Catch ya later. Get it?" I mumble. Delia huffs. "What do we do now?"

"I think we should take him to the hospital."

"What if he poofs someone?"

"I don't think he can anymore." Delia crouches next to Brigley. Fear races through my stomach. "Mr. Brigley, can you talk?"

The old man shivers and coughs before speaking so quietly I can hardly hear him. "Could you bring me a blanket, dear?"

"You shouldn't be on the floor, coach. Let's get you somewhere warmer." Delia lifts the man.

If you'd said she'd be able to carry Brigley an hour ago, I'd have laughed, but things sure have changed.

She carries the frail man to the sofa, covers him in blankets, then turns to me. "Will you call 911 on my phone, please? You remember how right? Tell them there's an old man at this address who fell and needs an ambulance. Do you remember the address?"

I nod. It makes the torn area of my neck hurt, and Delia looks concerned when I wince. I smooth my features as best as I'm able. "Yes, and yes. I'll call now."

I scramble to find her phone and stylus, and when I do I make my first phone call on a modern phone. The ambulance arrives surprisingly quickly and all the things they have in their vehicle are really impressive. I have to wonder how often people think about that sort of thing.

Mr. Brigley is taken to the hospital with sirens blaring at top volume. Delia calls Rosa while I attempt to tape my neck back together. I hope it heals. I hope I *can* heal.

"Did you get it? I can help," Delia says as she walks into the bathroom where I'm standing in front of the mirror, checking the finished job.

"No, thank you. I've got it. Just hope it works. Everything alright with Rosa?" I turn to her and set my hands on her waist.

Delia kisses the center of my forehead, then the tip of my nose. "Everything's just fine. She's calling to tell Angelo to bring the other stick of gum back to her. I don't know what she'll do with it. None of my business. Now we have to find the other girls."

The mango-chili lollipop Rosa made is supposed to help us find my teammates. I guess the way it'll work is when it's sweet, it'll mean we're far from the girls, and when it's spicy we're close. Hopefully, it works. If what happened to Brigley is any indication, then her spells should work just fine.

"Well, tomorrow, we can find them." I sigh. "I know we should find them now but it's night-time and I'm tired. Is it selfish to wait?"

Delia takes my hand and leads me to the bedroom. "We'll just get up early."

"*Pbfft*," Mavis says.

"I'm going to make Mavis an egg in the morning before we go."

Delia looks at me with a raised eyebrow. "Whatever you say."

Chapter Ten
Delia

Well, the charm worked. We found five tins and took them back to Rosa's. She shooed Brock—who I was surprised to see there—out of the store and closed up again.

"I'm sorry you have to keep closing because of us," I apologize.

"Don't worry. I work almost every day. A little time off won't kill me." She smiles as she arranges the tins on the countertop. "Now, let's try to wish these open. We may not be their true loves, but our hearts do desire their happiness."

Pearl, Rosa, Sharon, Angelo, and I each place our hands on top of a tin and wish for it to open, and for the girl inside to come out. We then step back and wait. Nothing happens.

"Sometimes magic happens best when no one is looking," Rosa says and indicates we should turn.

We all face the opposite direction. It seems silly to me that facing the other way would make a difference, but lo and behold, not thirty seconds later shocked exclamations ring out behind us.

Five women in baseball uniforms, all three-dimensional—unlike Pearl—sit on the counter, looking different levels of shocked and frightened. They whisper among themselves for a moment. One of the women, a very short, young, Latina woman with bleach-blonde hair, jumps off of the counter first and looks over us. Apparently deciding Rosa is the one in charge, she approaches her with a determined set to her jaw.

"You in charge here?" she asks. "I'm captain of these girls. We all got more than a few questions."

Rosa looks around at us, then shrugs. "You could say I'm in charge here. Your teammate, however, is more likely to be able to answer your questions."

I slide out of the way to reveal Pearl, who has been hiding behind me. She tries to shrink back again but I don't let her. When they see her, they gasp. Pearl waves awkwardly, her expression tight with nerves.

"Hi there. As you can see, I've had a little bit of trouble. You all are fine though, don't worry. Well, you've been locked in a box for almost eighty years." She shrugs. "But otherwise, you're fine."

The women all begin to ask questions at once. Apparently, finding out they've been zoomed most of a century into the future is just as tough for them to believe as it was for Pearl. She's patient and answers every question she can, and the ones she can't the rest of us fill in. It takes a long time, but we get to every one of them that we know the answer to. Angelo contacts a friend who owns an apartment complex with a couple places available who's willing to let the ladies stay there until they can get back on their feet. We all agree to do as much as we can to help them learn how to live these days, bring them things they need, etc. It'll be tough for a while, but they're all strong. I know they'll be fine.

As for Brigley, Pearl and I went to visit him in the hospital. He couldn't talk much. We asked the doctors what's wrong with him and, I guess, there isn't anything in particular. He's just...old. When we got rid of the curse, monster, experiment, or whatever it was that had taken him over, he returned to a normal, human guy who just so happens to be well over a hundred years old. I called the nursing home and sort of explained what happened. They said it's not the weirdest thing they've heard of, and they'd take care of everything. He'll have a place to stay.

The Wonder Balls are, unfortunately, done for the season. They're looking for a new coach and, while Mr. Brigley still technically owns the stadium, he can't efficiently make decisions. He also doesn't have a will or the capacity to make one. It will likely go to the city when he passes. What will happen then, I have no idea. The Wonder Balls will definitely still play—the towns folk would riot if they didn't—I just have no idea what things will look like when it's not under Brigley's rule.

As for The Wonder Belles? Information about them has been slowly reappearing now that they've returned—individual things like their birth records, photos in family albums etc., but also things that involve other people. News articles talking about The Wonder Belles have reappeared in the archives. The names of the lost girls are, sadly, gone for good. I think that'll take a while for the Belles to get over, and that's more than understandable. They do want to play again someday though, and I hope they do. I hope they get new women from all over as well.

Oh, and Pearl's movies are back. Which means her old public service films are back too. We found them—and they're hilarious. Pearl doesn't get why I couldn't stop laughing, but a whole thirty-minute movie telling teens that if they go past holding hands they'll never grad-uate was some kind of work coming from her. The drive-in is going to have a night to play old public service announcements and hers are def-initely going to be a major feature. She's being grumpy, but I for sure think she's excited to be a bit of a star again.

"Hey, Delia?" Pearl asks as we're out walk-ing to Kyle's to get a drink.

"What's up, Bubbles?"

She giggles at the nickname like she always does.

"I read on the Internet that they have little vibrators people can wear inside of them, and they can be controlled by another person from anywhere through their phone. Is that true?"

I stop and stare at her. "Where the hell have you been looking on the Internet? But anyway, yes, that's true Pearl."

"Wow. Phones really can do everything."

She starts to walk but I set my hand on her shoulder—which has healed, thank goodness—to stop her.

"Is that something you'd like?"

Pearl looks around us, and when she sees no one is there, tugs my nipple piercing through my thin tee-shirt. "I think I would."

I take her hand, turn the opposite direction and start walking at a brisk pace.

"Wait, aren't we going to Kyle's?" Pearl asks.

"Nope. I'm taking you to Carl's."

"Carl's? I've never heard anyone mention that place."

"Yeah. People don't, uh, usually mention going to places like Carl's, but that's definitely where we need to go."

We walk at a steady pace, arriving shortly at Carl's Adult Emporium. I tend to get my toys online, but when I want something now, Carl's will do. It's a little seedy, and the prices are higher than they should be, but they've always got what I need.

As soon as I open the door and Pearl sees what's inside, her face turns bright red. She might be sexually adventurous, but I don't think she's ever seen a wall of rainbow-colored, realistic, monster dick-shaped vibrators, or a giant, high-definition screen playing a pansexual, demon-kraken orgy. A Ghostlight Falls sex shop can't be beat.

"Alright, we should find at least a few of them to choose from over here," I say as I guide Pearl to the area where the remote vibrators are.

"Alright. That's good," she says as she drags her hand along a display of werecat pheromones. "Can we look around a bit too?"

"Anything you want," I say with a laugh.

Unfortunately, Brock appears around the corner, holding a magazine called Goth Girls with Huge Honkers and a tube-shaped item I quickly look away from before I can make out what it is. I think hard about baseball to bleach away this memory.

"Oh, uh, Dee," he mumbles. "Dee's girl. Hello."

"Don't make conversation in the sex shop, Brock. It's weird," I say, scooting past him.

He steps in my way. *What the fuck?*

"Uh, so, since we're both here, I'm just wondering if maybe I can ask a favor," he says in a kind of nervous stammer I've never heard from him. Pearl and I look at each other in confusion as he continues. "Can you mention me to Sharon? In a good way. Say I'm handsome or nice or something like that. But also, don't tell her I said to mention me."

For a moment I'm at a loss for words. Thankfully, Pearl isn't.

"Delia isn't a liar. She can tell Sharon how you're rude to her though, if you want. That all right?"

Brock's cheeks turn red as he scratches the back of his neck. "Forget it. See you later."

I wrap my arm around Pearl's waist as he walks away and when he's out of sight I kiss her. When she pulls away, she grins.

"Had to defend my girlfriend."

"Don't get too used to it. I'm capable of defending myself." I slap her backside, making her yelp and me laugh.

"Who's messin' with the magazines?" Carl, the owner, shouts from somewhere near the register. *Oops.*

"I think he's referring to my bottom," Pearl whispers.

"I think you're right, darling." We both break into laughter. Once we've calmed down, I take her hand again. "Now, let's get this thing."

On the walk home we wave to all the new people she's met, talk about life, and just enjoy each other's company. When we near Bertram's tree, this huge, old tree in a secluded area, on the edge of town, I pull her aside.

"What's going on?" she asks, as if something's wrong.

I flatten her back against the tree, one of my arms propped against it at a right angle. I kiss her deep and hard before breaking away.

"I love you so much. Say you'll stay with me," I plead.

"Are you sure you'll want me if Rosa can't fix me? I know we've been fine so far but there's been the hope she might be able to. But if she can't—"

I get as close as I can to her, so that if anyone comes along, they won't be able to see what's going on, and fold up her skirt. I tear her paper panties off and toss them to the side.

"Delia! What are you—"

"Pearl, no matter what happens, I want you. Any way that you are, that's how I want you." I force her legs apart and find the open slit of her cunt. I tease the opening, flipping my thumb over it like the pages of a book. She squirms beneath me. "Tell me you love me too."

"I do. I love you." I thrust my fingers inside her, pinning her against the old tree with my aching body, and licking along her neck. "Oh, God, I love you."

I press my mouth against her ear as I fuck my fingers fast inside her, already feeling the sugary build up inside her that I'm starting to recognize means I'm doing things right. I grin.

"Forever. You and me," I whisper. "My wonderful Wonder Belle."

Bonus Chapter

Brock

What the hell am I supposed to do? The stadium is closed. There isn't anywhere else in this stupid town I can practice. No one else even *wants* to practice. They're happy about the vacation. HAPPY about it. It's disgusting. They're all a bunch of loser beta males.

I finish my last push-up and chug the end of my protein shake. I've got nothing else to do today and it's only the middle of the afternoon. Baseball has been my life for...well, it's always been. I can't just sit around and twiddle my thumbs until the old man kicks the bucket, and they reopen.

I scoot my dog, Catcher, out of my favorite chair, and turn on the rarely used television. I'll watch some old training videos, keep my mind in the game at least. I search for the remote and find it hiding under the magazine full of naked goth chicks I got the other day. I know print is old-fashioned, but I've just never gotten into the whole Internet porn thing. Something about a glossy babe in my hands can't be replaced. Dee's got a live paper babe, I saw. Crazy stuff. Never know what's gonna happen around here.

I take a look at the chicks for a minute, but I gotta set the magazine down. My dick's barely hard and, honestly, I'm sad. I look at the golden retriever curled up at my feet and sigh.

"Catcher, how am I gonna make Sharon like me?"

He doesn't say anything because he's a dog.

"I'm gonna go to her store to see her."

Catcher huffs and it sounds frustrated, but I'm sure it's a coincidence.

I put on a nice, cropped Wonder Balls t-shirt and some low-sling sweatpants to show off my abs, lace up my fresh, white high-tops, and my wraparound shades. Then, I jump in my red convertible, and speed to Rosa's Dulcería.

I park in the closest spot to the front door. I think it's a disabled spot, but no one ever uses it.

They can just come inside and ask me to move if they need it. I will. I'm a reasonable guy.

I shut the car door, smooth my hair back in the rearview mirror, and make sure my teeth are still dazzlingly white. I paid a lot of money for these teeth to look this good, so I take care of them.

As soon as I open the door to Rosa's and lift my sunglasses, I see her: Sharon Cristina Silva y Pacheco. The most beautiful woman in the world.

"Go away," she says as she slaps a sticker on a bag of licorice.

Her black hair nearly covers her eyes, but I don't need to see it to know what expression she's making. I know her inside and out. I've been studying her since we were kids. Right now, she'll look the same as she almost always does—bored to death.

"Is that any way to speak to your favorite customer?" I reply leaning against the shelf nearest the registers so my shirt rides up nice and high.

I flex my abs and grin. A few things on the shelf fall somewhere, but I'm sure it's fine.

Sharon mumbles something, but it's too quiet for me to hear. I notice that she changed her hairstyle. I'll mention it with a compliment. Show that I care.

"I like your front hair today. Looks nice."

"My *front hair*? What the hell does that mean?"

"The hair in front." I hold my hand where my forehead is. *Hmm. There must be a girl word. Oh, right. I remember.* "You cut your bongs. Looks nice."

"Ugh. Something is wrong with you. What do you want?" She slaps another sticker on some licorice with enough force that her big knockers jiggle inside her black lace top. *Hell yeah.*

"I want something sweet, of course." I set my elbows on the counter and lean toward her. "But I want it very, very spicy."

"Ugh." She slaps a sticker over my mouth and walks away.

Rosa, her mom, walks out from the back room and sees me leaning there with a sticker over my mouth like a moron. She quirks her head to the side but smiles and waves anyway.

I peel the sticker off of my mouth and wave back. The sticker reads "Welcome Belles." I frown. Those must be gifts for the Wonder Belles. They're the reason I can't play baseball.

"Hello there, Mr. Baseball Pitcher. What would you like today?"

At least Sharon's mom is nice to me.

"He said he wants spicy candy," Sharon says to her. "Very, very spicy."

"Hmm. I don't want to sell him something too spicy. Maybe we just do some cinnamon or—"

"Hey mom." Sharon bumps Rosa with her elbow and points out the front windows. "Look at his car. Nice parking job, huh?"

I look out at my car to see what she's talking about. I guess I did a pretty good job. I'm right in the center of that blue rectangle. When I turn back to the ladies, they're both looking at me with huge grins.

"Very, very spicy it is," Rosa says. "A strong man like you can handle it, I'm sure."

I flex my bicep as she walks past, heading to the taffy wall. Rosa gives it a squeeze just as

I'd hoped. I've got this one in the bag. Won the mom over, now to win the girl.

Rosa opens the only taffy in a glass case and takes just one piece to the counter.

"One piece? That's all I get?"

"All you need," Rosa replies. "You just take a nibble and it's enough for a *normal* person."

I look over to Sharon, her arms crossed under her big, beautiful, bosom, waiting patiently for me to check out. I gotta make an impression on her.

"A normal person?" I scoff. "What about the handsome star pitcher of a leading minor league baseball team?"

"Oh, I don't know. Someone would have to be pretty strong to handle the spice level in this." Rosa scans the label on the taffy and pushes it toward me. "Two dollars."

I pull two crisp dollar bills out of my wallet and slide them to her before taking the taffy and tearing open the red and pink striped wax paper.

"I'm not afraid of a little spice." I wink at Sharon. "I'll take everything you got."

Rosa shakes her head and Sharon snorts as I toss the taffy in the air and catch it in my mouth.

As soon as I start to chew, I know I've made a terrible mistake.

My scalp feels like it's going to fly off. My nose starts to run. Tears stream from my eyes. I force my mouth to form the general shape of a smile as sweat leaks from every pore.

"Wow. It's really good," I say with air from lungs that feel like deflating balloons.

All of my muscles clench and my mouth starts to water uncontrollably. I manage to swallow much of the taffy, but I can't get it all. It keeps burning and burning like a Molotov cocktail because it's stuck in my teeth. My beautiful, expensive teeth.

I think I might puke.

"Wow, you're really strong, Brock. I'm impressed. Now you can leave and get out of the disabled spot. Thanks," Sharon says.

I wave as I back away, turn, then quickly exit. I can't speak to say goodbye or I'll hurl. I get in my car and speed away as fast as I can. It's still burning when I get home. I drink a ton of milk and brush my teeth until I can feel something other than pain in my mouth again.

I sit in my chair and turn on the television to watch some baseball before bed. I think back to the events at the candy store and smile. I reach down and scratch Catcher on his head.

"She was impressed by my strength, Catcher. She even said it. We'll be together in no time."

Thank You

Thank you so much to my beta readers. You keep me from a complete mental breakdown between the first draft and the final draft. I'd never get a thing published without you.

Thank you to Tee for helping me with all the miscellaneous things my brain can't deal with, and for continuing to talk sense into me once I have run out of my own. Thank you Alijay for helping me with newsletters; now I don't have to force the squirrel who runs my brain to learn how to do it. Thank you Latrexa for helping me appreciate storms again. Thank you, Cassie, for including me in things even when I continue to be the tornado whirling around your Kansas. Oz looks pretty when we get there though, doesn't it?

Read the Rest of the Series

Check out all the stories in the Ghostlight Falls
series:

The Totally Typical Tale of Mappy McMapface
Nicole Parker

Paper and Passion
Thea Masen

Romanced by the Rat
G.M. Fairy

Bread by the Grim
Dakota Cockaday

Want More?

Follow Ghostlight Falls on Instagram and follow me on any of my socials linked below for updates on the second season of books in the Ghostlight Falls series. You might even find out what exactly happens to Sharon when she cooks, what Angelo shifts into, and if Brock can stop being a douche.

https://sylviamorrow.carrd.co
https://www.instagram.com/ghostlightfalls